Luminous Mysteries

John Holman

Luminous Mysteries

HARCOURT BRACE & COMPANY

New York   San Diego   London

Requests for permission to make copies of any part
of the work should be mailed to: Permissions Department,
Harcourt Brace & Company, 6277 Sea Harbor Drive,
Orlando, Florida 32887-6777.

A version of "Immaterial" was published in *Forum*, the
Magazine of the Florida Humanities Council, in 1993. "Power
Burgers" and "Rita's Luminous Mystery" were both published
in *The Oxford American*. "Why They Named the Baby Lake"
was published in *Fiction*, May 1998. "Damaged Luxury"
was published in *The Mississippi Review*, June 1998.

Library of Congress Cataloging-in-Publication Data
Holman, John, 1951–
Luminous mysteries/John Holman.—1st ed.
p.   cm.
ISBN 0-15-100349-1
I. Title.
PS3558.035593L86   1998
813'.54—dc21   98-20997

Text set in Granjon
Designed by Lori McThomas Buley
Printed in the United States of America
First edition
E D C B A

For Carmen, Alea, and Jonathan

Contents

Luminous Mysteries

Touring

THEIRS WAS A rural community tucked away from the city. A four-lane intersection with a stoplight protected their neighborhood's timeless character from office buildings, fast-food restaurants, traffic, and white people. Fathers had built dirt-surface basketball courts, taught the kids softball, given them bicycles, buried the dead pets. They worked as mechanics, gardeners, bricklayers and farmers. One sold insurance, maybe one was in jail or prison, some were Korean War veterans, some were dead, and some, like Grim's father, were missing.

The neighborhood had changed. Many longtime residents had died, and their children had moved away, taking the grandchildren with them. Many of the old houses were now rental properties—cheaply and sloppily painted purple and white, orange and brown, marigold and blue —and oddly dull. One of the houses actually improved, as if restored to a pride known before the former owners became too sick and too old to plant flowers in the yard, to replace a faded awning, to repair a sagging porch. More often the renters, people from who knew where, move out of gutted, littered husks. Strange people in strange cars rolled up and down the streets.

The liquor house became a drug house. The new economy, Rita, Grim's sister, mused. Bonnie's place, now that Bonnie was dead, was run by her son. He sold more heroin than booze and used the house not to make a profit, as Bonnie had done, but to earn a nod. Neighbors warned Rita. Neighborhood boys had started going to Bonnie's to shoot and snort smack. But the boys were older than Grim, seventeen at least. And Rita kept Grim too busy. Weekends and summers he was at camps—art, karate, basketball, science. She'd sent him to private schools in town since nursery school.

After their father left, Rita became Grim's guardian. Their mother had died in a car crash when Grim was four and Rita was nineteen. Two years later their father, who traveled the East with cases of cigarette samples, went on a trip and never came back. So Rita had pretty much been a parent despite one of them always reminding the other that she was certainly not Grim's mother. Also, she taught math and was studying for her master's. These responsibilities gave her both community nobility and the disposition of a boss.

Still, she cried often, in her sleep. The cry would start low and rise in volume and pitch, a ghostly, frightening wail to Grim. She didn't cry every night, but sometimes she screamed Grim's name. At first she wouldn't tell him what she dreamed, but later she did, after he started teasing and mimicking her. Someone was chasing her, and then him, or they were falling. Often, Rita was straining to reach Grim and snatch away syringes that bristled from his long thin body. Eventually, because he asked her, she told him everything. She remembered everything.

When he had holidays or a free weekend she took him to the college where she taught, or on shopping errands for some elderly person who hadn't left the area. Some nights they went to meetings of the school board or the board of aldermen where they sat in the audience and Rita spoke out against harmful school closings and zoning laws. That's where she met Mayes, her boyfriend, who taught high-school physics and raised his own voice against changes he thought would hurt the neighborhoods. Mayes lived in the city, where urban renewal was turning the streets of his students into a ghetto, just as flight to and from those streets was making a scar of Rita's community.

Most nights Rita liked to sit on the porch. From her slant she watched a group of young men gather across and up the street. They stood near a dull fire hydrant in front of a tree-filled vacant lot, drank quart bottles of beer and smoked. The lot's owner had installed a light on a pole on which he'd nailed No Trespassing signs. The boys pulled the signs down, and the owner put them back up, climbing taller on a ladder to post them out of reach. The boys stood on each other's shoulders to snatch them, and the pole was dotted with stapled corners of thin red cardboard. These were some of the boys who drifted to and from Bonnie's. During the winter they rolled a rusted oil drum to the spot and built orange-yellow fires, tilted up beer bottles to send quick tracers of firelight from their dark fingers. Some of the boys should have been in Rita's math classes by now, but none of them was likely to go to college. She thought this as she sat shivering in her overcoat covering her flannel pajamas, and smoked her cigarettes. She hoped the cold would freeze their brains to clarity. When spring came they were still there, eyes like moons, feeding her dreams.

One Saturday that spring Rita woke to the sound of a lawnmower, the first of the season. Its sudden, urgent whine lifted her out of sleep. The first thing she saw was the white-blooming Bradford pear tree filling her bedroom window. The window was a large and A-shaped attic window. The tree had opened full overnight. She was in such a good mood she slipped out to the store to buy melons and berries for breakfast.

When Grim came into the kitchen, she poured batter onto the waffle iron. He had been in his room practicing rope tricks, spinning small loops to hop in and out of, and lassoing his bedposts, the straight-back chair and the floor lamp with the Western-scene shade. He watched steam issue from the waffle iron and noted Rita's happiness. It seemed extraordinary. She had been sad lately, and now she was grinning and sliding about the kitchen in her socks, way beyond her normal good mood. He saw his bicycle by the opened back door and realized she'd been riding it. Maybe, because of her mood, she'd agree to drop him off alone at a movie.

But Rita told him of her plan to visit Mrs. Pack for lunch. Mrs. Pack had been Grim's preschool teacher, and her husband, Kip, had just gotten out of the hospital. He'd nearly been killed in a fight with his grandnephew, who had broken into their trailer. The luncheon was to cheer up Kip and to thank Rita for cooking a few meals, washing loads of clothes, and taking some bills to the post office during the ordeal.

Once on the long dirt road to the Packs', Grim drove. He was twelve. During the winter, they had spent cold, dry Sundays on deserted two-lanes, Grim driving the Cutlass, Rita acting as if his driving was a novelty. But he knew how to drive. Soon Rita would settle into the routine—peering into the woods for cardinals and deer, hoping to glimpse lovers hiking over leaf mounds.

The woods on the way to the Packs' were filled with floating pink and white dogwoods and wafting veils of wisteria. Wisteria traced the old wooden arch over the entrance to the Packs' rutted driveway. "Slow down," Rita said, grinning and bouncing.

Kip sat at one of two white-draped card tables set up in the tall spring grass. The closer they got, the more things swayed—the grass, the skirts of the tablecloths, the trailing vines of the willow under which Kip sat.

They jostled to a stop in front of Kip, beside the Packs' shiny brown Chrysler parked along the honeysuckle vines covering the property-line fence. Kip was still bandaged, his arms and right hand swathed in padded gauze. His eyes were bruised. He wore a brown-and-blue plaid short-sleeved shirt buttoned formally at the neck. A translucent pitcher of lemonade—circles of lemon slices floating—glowed on the table with four, ice-filled daisy-printed glasses. He had suffered broken ribs, a punctured lung, a concussion, and multiple cuts. He had fought off the grandnephew with only one leg, because diabetes had already claimed the other one. But today he had a new prosthesis under his stiffly starched khakis. He slowly turned a knobby, thickly shellacked cane by his knee as he smiled at Rita's and Grim's approach. Black, buglike stitches traced his upper lip.

Rita said, "Kip, the valiant. Home again." She hugged him and kissed his cheek. He had shaved unevenly, patches of white stubble under his nose and on his jaw and chin.

"I'm a shell of the man I used to be, darlin'."

"Oh, really? Oh my, what a shell."

"Heh-heh." He looked at Grim. "Hey, boy." He held out his left, unbandaged hand, and Grim met it with his right hand. Grim grasped Kip's over the top and they shook that way, awkwardly, as if building shaky team spirit.

"Lemonade?" Kip asked, as he fanned flies from the mouth of the pitcher.

Mrs. Pack came out the trailer door carrying a foil-covered bowl. "Potato salad," Kip said.

"Your old man looks great," Rita called out.

"I don't itch," Kip said.

"Yeah? I guess he looks O.K.," Mrs. Pack said. She was barefoot, a tall woman in bluer-than-natural denim pants, the polyester kind with white stitching. Her sky blue sleeveless knit top exposed heavy, muscular arms and hands. She placed the bowl on the table and turned to hug Rita.

"You could give him the palpitations on top of all else. So young and little and smelling good. He's suffered enough," she said, laughing.

"Shell of a man," Kip said.

She hugged Grim. Sweat already beaded up through her too-tan makeup. She wore red lipstick and rouge. She had shaved, too.

In preschool, her shaving bothered Grim. At the end of the day he was usually the last kid stranded. Rita was always late, often from a meeting at the high school where she taught then, or from a class she was taking. On very late days, Mrs. Pack either couldn't wait any longer or couldn't think of anything else to do, or maybe she had to get ready for an engagement of her own—so she left the bathroom door open to keep an eye on Grim while she draped a striped towel over her shoulder and shaved. She lathered up with a brush and bar of soap, squared her sideburns and carefully down-stroked her chin and cheeks. Grim thought he shouldn't have to see that. Mrs. Pack frowned with distaste, too. She'd wipe her face with the towel and turn to him. She kept the sink's faucet running while she spread a pink cream over her lip. She'd grimace, and then try to smile at Grim.

Rita went with Mrs. Pack to the trailer to fetch more food. Grim sat with Kip and asked about the guinea hens they kept in a pen out back. Usually, out of boredom, he would walk behind the trailer to look at them, and he was anticipating doing so soon.

"We lost a couple," Kip said. "Just last night. Weasel."

"Weasel?"

"Pop goes it."

Grim worried about what Kip meant for a second. Kip rolled his eyes upward and shook his head, as if Grim's silence was sympathy. "A real weasel?" Grim asked.

"Weasels everywhere. Maybe it was a fox. But weasels like guineas."

"I've never seen a real weasel. They live around here? How come I never saw one?"

"Sam saw it."

Sam was their dog, a small old tan-and-black breed they kept tied to the willow. His face was on the ground behind the tree trunk. The most Grim had seen Sam do was sneeze.

"He yapped at it," Kip said. "We came out here with him straining on that rope, guineas squawking. Lola got the shotgun but the thing was gone. Two birds, too." He fanned a couple of flies from the pitcher. "Brand-new shotgun. Just got it," no doubt suspecting Grim was wondering about the break-in, like why they hadn't shot the grandnephew.

Rita and Mrs. Pack returned with covered platters. "Fried chicken, corn on the cob, greens, a little roast pork, macaroni and cheese," Kip said. "Pie later." They set the platters on the second table, which had paper plates stacked in the center.

"It's got hot out here. Pour yourself some of that lemonade," Mrs. Pack said to Grim. "Or do you want a beer?"

"No, ma'am," Grim laughed with her. "Too early."

"Rita? You? Me and Kip about give up strong drink. But we still got beer. Kip can't have none."

"You've been trying to get Grim drunk since he was a

baby," Rita said. She peeked under the foil cover of one platter and did a double take at the fried chicken. The pepper on it was moving. She looked again. Her thoughts had been racing all morning, and it could have been her own mind making the pepper skitter. She checked the sliced pork, and its pepper moved, too. She realized she was looking at ants. The greens—she looked closely at the dark wet folds, almost took some comfort in them—swarmed with ants.

"Mrs. Pack, we've got a lot of little problems here. We can't eat this."

"What, honey? Why not?" She saw the ants, and she put her big hands to her rouged cheeks and rubbed hard, a raspy sound. "Lord, Kip, what happened? I cooked all this food and we can't use it."

"It would have been good, too," Rita said. "You're such a great cook."

"Them ants sure love it."

Grim laughed. Rita looked at him, disapproval in the tilt of her head.

"And I've been nibbling all morning," Mrs. Pack said. "You reckon I been eating ants? Sheesh." She made her look of distaste, her lips twisting as when she watched herself shave.

"Ants are good food. Ants can't hurt you. But watch out for fly legs, though." Kip fanned the pitcher.

"I'm so sorry," Mrs. Pack said.

"It's all right." Rita put her hand on Mrs. Pack's broad back. "We can go get something. Go out."

Mrs. Pack looked to Sam lying on the ground. She stomped. "Damn good-for-nothing dog."

"It's not his fault, is it?" Grim asked.

"Hot dogs, it is," Rita said. "When's the last time you had a good hot dog?"

"You get yourself a fly leg and you got yourself trouble," Kip explained. "It'll gripe you good."

"Oh, Kip. Pour the damn lemonade. Hush with that old folk lie. Always got some fake wisdom when you ought to be helping keep ants off my food."

"Ain't no lie, honey. For me, though, it's unusual to regurgitate. Now my sack ain't iron, but if something disagrees with me, say like a fly leg, what happens is it turns my bowels into a cauldron—a boiling cauldron—but regurgitate, no."

They decided to leave the food on the tables, to leave it for whatever animals wanted it. Mrs. Pack went to get her shoes and to lock up the trailer. Rita poured lemonade over the melting ice in the glasses. She was conscious of the sun lighting everything. She was thinking so fast she felt she could almost catch the light before it shone in the pouring stream of lemonade.

Grim rode with Kip in the back of the Packs' Chrysler. "We're in a cloud in here," he said, feeling hardly a bump on the ruts and rocks of the driveway and dirt road. "This car is great."

Kip smiled at him. Grim settled into the soft leather corner and watched spring scroll by.

Rita wished she was somewhere else—home with the clean coral red kitchen countertops their father had installed before she was born. She wanted to gaze out at the pear tree, breathe its musky scent. This morning it had looked like a fat, suspended snowfall outside her bedroom

window. She thought about Mayes, whose hair was turning prematurely white. He was only thirty-three, two years
older than she was. Now, she would rather have been
breathing that tree with him than in Mrs. Pack's atrocious
car. It was a huge ostentatious gas hog, inappropriate for
a woman living in a rotting, ant-infested trailer. Mrs. Pack
had gone blind or crazy, and Rita didn't want to be
around that decline right now—not when her tree was
blooming, not when she was forgetting the crumbling of
her own neighborhood.

Mrs. Pack, adoring as she was, was often the object of
Rita's and Grim's jokes. They laughed about her shaving,
her wood-chopping strength. They wondered if she wasn't
a man. When they learned she and Kip had survived the
violent break-in, Rita had said, "Well, that was a very close
shave."

"Yeah," said Grim. "Despite the hairs on their chinny
chin-chins."

Mayes was at the house. Rita and Grim were laughing
and trying to eat sliced-turkey sandwiches. He said, "Show
some respect. They have faced enough. You know it's been
rough on them."

Rita snickered. They sprawled laughing all over the
kitchen.

From Grim's seat beside Kip, he saw her smile. He
wondered if Rita had noticed a small glass eye stuck in
the shiny handle of the cypress cane Kip kept tucked to
his plastic thigh, but Rita was staring out the window.
Grim gazed down at the cane.

"It's a seeing-eye stick," Kip exclaimed. "Huh? Pretty
ain't it? Strong and light. A friend of mine made it. It

can see for me, see? Heh-heh." He brushed his thumb over the thick pupil.

Rita turned to look into the backseat. Kip held up the stick. " 'Cause I'm a shell of the man." Rita smiled. The stick was hideous.

She thought about her early days with Mayes when he used to press her against brick walls and kiss her neck. The first time, they had gone to a math-and-science conference in St. Augustine. After the closing banquet they walked the short beach behind the hotel where stray gulls and herons scavenged along the broken seawall. When he escorted her back to her door, he leaned in to her and kissed her. He was heavy and warm. He touched her face. He smelled like citrus and smoke. The next morning he sent a poem to her room, a stanza about his pressing against her, their palms together, and a strutting, white, long-necked bird pulling the beach as if it were a foaming blue cape. There was a gold moon with glittering minarets spinning around it, and light coursing through their bodies in the wild bent pattern of lightning

She was feeling that lightning now. She felt charged, ready to leap out of the car. A pretty glade was going by, a couple of quick, black-winged yellow birds zipping low to the ground.

Kip said, "Now that's a beautiful property, tied up in court right now. But, boy, can't you imagine a double-wide set back up in there?"

Much later Rita told Grim what she had been thinking then. She had long wanted Grim to become an architect, maybe build Mayes's city ringing the moon, and Kip's dream about a double-wide was both ludicrously diminishing and touchingly sincere. She wanted to haul Grim away from there at the same time as she wanted him to value what Kip and Lola Pack were.

It didn't take long to get to town. Mrs. Pack parked in a small open-air municipal lot. Approaching Main Street, Rita moved with her usual quick purpose, her thick pony-tail swinging. Mrs. Pack pointed out the Korean-run wig shops in the old Woolworth and Walgreen buildings. "Everything's different." Kip and Grim lagged behind, Kip not used to his new leg. At one point he stopped, made the leg bend, and picked up a penny from the ground. "That's why I'm lucky. My good-for-shit nephew is too dumb and lazy to bend for a penny. You didn't think an old man like me could do it, did you?"

Percussive music with very high treble seemed to block the sidewalk ahead of them. Two smiling brown, silk-haired women—one with the red dot on her forehead and both in saris—stood on the sidewalk by a rack of brilliantly colored silk scarves. Sandalwood perfumed their doorway. Next door was the Western shop where Grim had a fringed, buckskin jacket on lay-a-way. He wondered now if he might exchange it for one of the spring Stetson straw hats on window display, or a pair of the hand-tooled boots propped by the bale of hay.

The hot-dog place Rita remembered no longer sold hot dogs; the new people served grinders. There were five customers, all at one table. A woman came from the back with four menus and offered smoking or nonsmoking. Mrs. Pack couldn't understand what exactly a grinder was, what she would be eating She looked to Kip, who shrugged, as if to remind her he was a shell of the man he used to be.

"Maybe we'll come back," Rita said. "We're touring."

She giggled. They did look like tourists, she thought. Grim had on a red-and-white seersucker shirt and khaki pants. He and Kip wore clean white tennis shoes. Mrs. Pack had changed her jeans for white pants, and Rita wore a yellow checked jumper and carried a straw pocketbook. They were taking spring seriously, way too clean and pressed for downtown, where absolutely nothing was happening.

Kip had another idea for where to find hot dogs. Back on the street a police car cruised by, followed by a short line of creeping cars. From a red GTO a dark fat kid yelled, "Hey, Mr. Kip, I hear you had a heart attack!"

Kip yelled back, "It wasn't no heart attack!"

"Do I look like I had a heart attack?" he asked Mrs. Pack.

"It was a fight!" he yelled again to the kid in the car.

The kid was one of Rita's students, a slickster who signed his papers "Belly Man" and who had to be reminded to remove his hat in class. He made decent grades. He slumped now way down in the driver's seat, which was leaned so far back that his thick head was visible through the back passenger window. He winked at Rita.

"Now there's a hot dog," Mrs. Pack said.

"Taking that gangster lean too far," Rita said.

"I bet he rolls like a muntain," Mrs. Pack whispered to Rita.

"I'll bet so, too." Rita laughed.

"O.K., that's it," Kip said. "All the action for the day."

They made it to Mint Street and stood at an interaction across from a mirrored one-story building. It had green-striped awnings and a lit red neon sign: All Points Grill.

"Frankfurters?" Grim asked.

"Could be."

"What did it used to be, Kip?" Mrs. Pack asked.

"I sort of remember it," Rita said. "Always a restaurant, right, Kip?"

"You know I ain't what I was," Kip said, now disavowing his own idea.

Rita and Mrs. Pack rolled their eyes.

Their wavering reflections grew from small to large as they all approached the mirrored windows. Mrs. Pack hesitated at the door. "This looks like another white folks' place." But Rita went on in.

It was a white folks' place, mostly. Frazzled, worn-out-looking drunks sat at round and square tables. Nobody had food on the table. Everybody was drinking sixteen-ounce cans of beer. A Patsy Cline record lamented achingly from the jukebox. An interracial couple—white man, black woman—hunched over Pabst cans at a square two-seater catching sun at the wide window. They had seen Rita's party coming. But could they have thought they would come in? Or cared? This place was for sockless, shoelaceless people who smoked too-short cigarettes pinched to their lips.

From behind the bar a white-aproned black man with long nappy sideburns barked. "Nemo!"

Near the door a despondent-looking redheaded white man came to sudden life. He scrambled to clear cans and plastic cups from a table for four. He pulled a white towel from inside his thin yellow shirt and wiped down the tabletop, then scuttled around to pull back the wooden chairs. He slapped the seats with the towel and jerked his hand at Rita.

Nemo brought over narrow, red laminated menus. He hovered there holding a pad and pencil until the barman called "Nemo" again. He pivoted away, stuffed the pad into his back pocket and began clearing empties from other people's tables.

The menu featured regular dogs, chili dogs, and foot-longs; plus chuck wagons, fresh frozen fish fillets, famous burgers, chicken sandwiches, and soup de jour.

"They got stuff," Kip said, pleased.

Rita looked around with an odd expression of dazed excitement, as if a new kind of happiness was about to erupt. Something about the place, the smell maybe—body odor, beer, grease—or the filmy light through the mirrored windows, was making her smile so hard she could have been biting something.

"Are you O.K.?" Grim asked her.

"Man, this is some place," she said, the sound coming from deep in her throat.

A huge industrial floor fan oscillated against one wall. Rita could feel the buzz in her veins, as if the atoms of her blood vibrated. She felt as if she were riding in a fast-ascending elevator, a sudden emptiness in her stomach. She was quietly amazed that she was sitting still, grinning at the notion that nothing but the blades of the fan was moving much at all.

Kip's eyes suddenly hurt her. They were rheumy as egg yolks, like the other customers'. With his bandages and the damaged quality of the drinkers' faces, he looked like he belonged there. Mrs. Pack stared at the menu with tired age in her eyes. The black woman by the window had a bandaged ear—cotton gauze held with strips of clear tape. A white man at the bar wore a dirty unsigned arm cast. He had a hump in his back.

"Whoo, this place is on fire," Rita said, catching a note near to her nightmare wail.

Nemo was back with his pad, and Rita dazzled with questions. "What kind of meat is a chuck wagon?"

"Ma'am?"

"Your chilly dogs caught in the same frozen lake as your fish cubes?"

"Huh?"

"How long is your footlong?"

He held up his hands. "About this long."

"Let me see it. Never mind—what's so chicken about your sandwiches? What are they afraid of? What despicable things do you do to them, make them do? And just what is your soup de jour?"

"Oh, well, see we don't have no soup de jour today."

Rita laughed as if it was the funniest thing she had heard. "You don't?"

"We had it yesterday."

"Jesus Lord God Christ," Rita said, standing up, looking much too wide-eyed.

"Rita, what's the matter?" Grim asked.

She knew she didn't mean it, that she was acting like someone else. She was just thinking and feeling things so fast. "*You're* a famous burger, my friend," she said to Nemo. She sat, surprised to be breathing hard.

Kip and Mrs. Pack stared at her. Then, when Rita was quiet, grinning, Kip told Nemo to bring a round of dogs and sweet iced tea.

These sad drunks, Rita thought. Those moon-eyed boys

at home. She was trying to make her eyes as wide as theirs, late-night by the barrel fire. "What are they looking at, Grim?" She took his hand and stroked it. Her face relaxed, her eyes going soft. "I want to see it for you."

"Oh, Grim," she said, deep in love with him now, Patsy Cline's jukebox sadness soaking her heart. "That's not your name, sweetheart."

"Sis." He looked anxiously at her, and then at Kip and Mrs. Pack. They looked anxious, too.

"This is all so real right now," Rita said, laughing, her mood changing again. Her hand was like a soft machine on the back of Grim's hand. "I'm feeling sick, honey. I have to tell you that. Things are not exactly right; I know that. But it is so much more real." She looked at him tenderly, like a mother, or a lover, her eyes not letting him go.

"You are the most beautiful boy. I want to roll you up inside and keep you there." She held him a few seconds longer, then quickly released him.

"Maybe I swallowed that fly leg, stupid thing." She laughed. She got up from the table and headed for the bathroom. Her ponytail swung like a snapped cable as she pushed through the bathroom door.

"She'll be all right," Mrs. Pack said. "I'll go see about her in a minute."

"Your sister is a saint, boy. You can see that, I hope."

"Well," Mrs. Pack said, "doing everything she does. Does she sleep?"

Grim ignored them. This had happened before, a few years ago. He remembered how she had seemed to him then, as two Ritas, one inexactly laid over the other. Their aunt Ruth had to come take care of him then, and soon Rita had come back, after how long? A stay in a hospital, and he had forgotten to be afraid, and now he was again. Mayes should be here, he thought, angry at him. He hoped she would bring herself back in focus in the bathroom, but knew it couldn't happen like that. And soon he would have to go in and get her—not Mrs. Pack.

Rita leaned over the commode and watched the porcelain's atoms shimmy, wondering what was taking so long joking for the fly's leg to leap on out of her. She had to get Grim out of there. She had things to do, people to pee, she said to herself. If things didn't happen as fast as she saw them she was going to burst, bloating as she was, float up and burst, disperse in a spray of sparks. She needed to calm down and see Mayes. He could help. He'd see immediately that something was wrong, that this was the happiest she had been in years.

Rocks

RITA COULDN'T TAKE IT. When Grim was thirteen, he overheard her on the phone talking with neighbors about a shoot-out and drug bust in another part of town, at the Hell's Angels' former local headquarters which had later burned down. It had been in the papers. Now they had to put up with the ones who hadn't been shot or arrested, she said.

Large, long-bearded, tattooed men stared from loud, chopped motorcycles as neighbors waited in the turn lane for the light to change. Sometimes a bike would roar by

Grim's house with a booted, tight-jeaned girl leaning on the back. Country-and-western music twanged and whined at odd hours. Beer cans and Jack Daniel's bottles littered the woods beside Grim's house. When the Hell's Angels rode for supplies, they drove a scraped, blue pickup with a Shoot Your Local Sheriff decal on the back bumper and a Confederate flag insignia on the front plate. But the decal that frightened Grim the most boasted that the only way they'd give up their guns would be to have them pried from their cold dead fingers.

Rita phoned and berated the real-estate company that managed Mr. Brown's house, accusing them of racism, of purposely guiding the Hell's Angels to a black neighborhood instead of a white neighborhood. Then she called Mr. Travis, the scoutmaster, retired by then, since about the only merit badges anyone could afford to earn were for hiking and knot-tying. He went downtown to talk with the property managers. He wore his tan gabardine suit, and later stood with his hat in his hand on Grim's doorstep, looking sheepish and resigned, more afraid of Rita than of the Hell's Angels or the white people downtown. The Hell's Angels, he said, had a lease.

A few of the boys decided to get rid of them. They gathered up some rocks and took the old, grown-over path through the woods. The house had stood empty for a year after Mr. Brown had finally died of bone cancer. It was the biggest house in the neighborhood, built of stone and wood and sitting on a hill of balding, scraggy yard. His mailbox had been a perfect target when he was alive. Boys would sling rocks at it until somebody banged it loud enough to set them running low and deeper into the woods. Now, crouched together behind the summer leaves of ground scrub, they could see the blue pickup and low-slung bikes parked in front of the house. Just across the dirt road, the mailbox still looked as big as a small dog-house, dented and rusted, all but a few flakes of red worn from the flag, the whole supported by a thick shaft of cornered wood.

"They could kill us," Lydell whispered.

"They can't do anything," Grim said. "Except take the hint."

"They can't kill us. How are they gonna know it's us?" Dwight's breath smelled of tuna, which Grim figured he had just eaten for lunch. "Mr. Brown never knew."

"He knew," Grim said.

No Hell's Angels were visible.

"He was a good guy, though," Dwight said. "He never called the cops or anything."

"What are they doing in there?" Grim asked.

Lydell shifted some rocks from one hand to another. "Gang-banging."

"Getting high," Dwight mumbled.

"They could take it out on the whole community." Lydell's round face looked stricken with awe by his prediction.

"Shit," Grim said. "We came here for a reason. Get the damn box."

Nobody moved. Dwight said, "But that's Mr. Brown's box."

It looked sad. The lip fit crookedly and the wooden pole listed to one side. Grim felt bad for ever having rocked it. But he had to give the Hell's Angels a message. "Throw them," he commanded.

Lydell stood up and threw one. It thumped up some dust in the ditch, too far from the mailbox for him to have been trying to hit it.

"It's been awhile," he said. "You go."

Grim was scared, but he was disgusted by Lydell's fake throw. He chose a heavy round rock that balanced fine in his fingers. He threw it hard and hit the wood post. It sounded a loud knock, and they crouched lower, backing up some.

After awhile, when no one came out of the house, Grim nudged Dwight. His rock put a new dent near the top of the box. Then Grim hit it square on the side, and Lydell, throwing straight this time, dusted off the rusting flag. They went belly down on the ground. One of the Hell's Angels came out the front door with a rifle. They dropped the rest of the rocks and ran.

That night, Grim told Rita, so that when the houses started to burn she'd be prepared. He took it as a responsibility, and as he made the decision he felt his scalp tighten, as if his skull had suddenly grown. He knew telling Rita was also an admission to the earlier stonings of the mailbox—when Mr. Brown would go door-to-door accusing kids—but that didn't matter in these extraordinary circumstances. He told her about the rifle, and she got angry. She said what he had done was cowardly, stupid, ignorant and wrong. Grim was stunned. They were in her bedroom, which had been their parents' bedroom. She put down the magazine she'd been reading and sat up on the edge of the bed. Grim looked around the room at anything but her scowling face, passing his eyes over old photographs of his mother and father, and of grandparents he never knew. A large bottle of fingernail-polish remover and a box of Kleenex were by the phone on the right end table. He saw himself in the mirror over the dressing table, and he looked ridiculous pinned against the bureau by her yelling.

She said those people had a legal and moral right to live there, that he could've gotten hurt, that he was no more than a criminal, that he wasn't too big for a whipping, that if he ever did that again he would get the beating of his life. Then she told him to go to bed.

He didn't sleep right away. It was still early for one thing. And he was trying to figure out whether or not he had been betrayed by his sister. She could get angry about the Hell's Angels but he wasn't allowed to. Despite what Rita had said, he knew he wasn't stupid. And he concluded that indeed he was brave. He had stoned the Hell's Angels' mailbox. How dare she call him a coward?

He dreamed that he walked through the screen door into the kitchen to find Rita playing cards with their mother and their mother's two sisters. Everyone was glad to see his mother, as though it was natural for her to be visiting from the dead. They were laughing and beautiful, not really playing cards, but reaching to touch each other's faces and hands while they talked. His mother wore lipstick and a sleeveless blouse. She didn't acknowledge that he was there. He couldn't hear what they said to each other, and they seemed to share some tender secret. But he didn't get it. "Where's Daddy?" he asked his mother. He said that when he had tried to phone her, he could hear her voice but he couldn't make her hear him. It seemed as though he really had tried to phone her. They didn't look at him. Their skin was moist. "What is it?" he said. "What's the truth about me?" His mother looked in his direction with the same smile she was sharing with the others, and then she turned back to playing cards.

He hardly spoke to Rita the next day. He made his own breakfast, washed his own dishes, and met Dwight and Lydell at the basketball court. They were playing one-on-one at the hoop that wasn't bent. He lay his bike next to theirs and got Dwight's rebound. He told them how Rita had acted.

"Man, that *was* stupid. You didn't tell her about us, I hope," Dwight said.

"We have to get them again today."

"He's crazy," Lydell said to Dwight. He looked at Grim. "What about your sister? Plus, the Hell's Angels will *blast* us."

"Not one person has told them to take a hike. We're the only ones who've got their attention." Grim launched a set shot at the far basket and watched the ball slip cleanly through the lopsided hoop. It was the longest shot he'd ever made, he realized. But he did not smile. He felt angry and proud—powerful.

They started loading up with rocks from around the basketball court. From the distance came the sound of thunder. But the thunder wouldn't stop. It was a deep grumble that grew louder, closer, and consuming, as a line of some fifty bikers came riding into the neighborhood. The sound drowned out everything else; no use trying to talk. The bikers filed one after the other down the road, revving their engines, until finally, bringing up the rear, cruised a crowded, muddy, green Cadillac with New

York tags, pulling a U-Haul trailer. The engines grumbled down June Road, the dirt road that led to the Hell's Angels' house. Slowly the roar diminished.

"This is your fault, Grim," Dwight said. "Now they're gonna kill the whole neighborhood."

"Hush," Grim said, but he no longer knew what to do with his rocks.

"They got enough people now to take on the whole police force. What's to stop them?"

Grim watched neighbors who had been witnessing the procession go back inside their houses. He listened for the sound of more bikes, but the road was quiet. "Let's check it out."

"*Are* you crazy?" Lydell said.

"Come on."

They left their bicycles at the court and walked with rock-stuffed pockets past the entrance to June Road. They ducked into the woods, crouched to the spot across from the mailbox, and saw a crowd of burly men and halter-wearing women standing around their bikes, talking and drinking beer. The rocks dug into Grim's thigh as he squatted. He sat down to unload them into a pile.

"Suppose we miss and hit one of those bikes?" Lydell asked.

"That'd piss them off," Dwight countered.

"Suppose we hit one of *them*," Lydell said.

"Let's just call the National Guard," Dwight said.

"This isn't a riot," Grim explained.

"Not yet," Dwight replied.

"We have to take care of this ourselves."

"Dammit, Grim, we're kids," Lydell whispered. "Have you noticed that?"

"Well, Lydell, that's why we only have rocks." He picked up one and threw it. It glanced off the thick seam along the top of the mailbox, making a dull, scraping thud. Two Hell's Angels looked up briefly but went back to talking. He threw again, a big one, and as soon as he released it Lydell grabbed his pants leg to pull him down. The rock hit the front of the mailbox and caved in the door. The sound was like an empty oil drum dropped on concrete.

This time the two Hell's Angels who had heard the first rock walked down the driveway to the mailbox. They examined the box and scooped up some of the stones that lay in the dirt. They started slinging them back through the woods, hitting tree limbs and tearing leaves all around Grim. One of them yelled, "My *name* is Rock!" When he came onto the road, peering, Dwight turned and ran. Lydell and Grim set out low behind him, whipped by the thin switches on the saplings.

They came out of the woods beside Grim's house. His heart knocked against the rocks remaining in his shirt pocket. He tried to look through the woods to see if anyone had followed, but all he could see were the woods. "Be quiet," he said to Dwight and Lydell, but all they were doing was breathing. From the woods, only bird noises. Then the loud twang of a country guitar wailed as the Hell's Angels cranked up the record player.

"You guys better go home," Grim said.

"What about our bikes?" Dwight said.

"Later."

The Hell's Angels played music loud all day. Grim stayed inside helping Rita clean. One of the aunts he had dreamed about was due in from Charlotte that evening, and they were straightening the house for her visit. He used the buffer to take his mind off the morning. After he had buffed the floors in the living room and the guest bedroom, he sat down in the kitchen and had some of the lemon Kool-Aid Rita had made. She pulled up a chair. She placed the dust cloth and the bottle of red furniture polish she was holding beside the Kool-Aid pitcher, and sipped from his glass.

"I guess you heard all those motorcyles this morning," he said.

"Who could miss them?"

"It's too many of them, now. I saw them."

"I figured that."

"What do you think that's about?"

She stared toward the kitchen window. "Sounds like they're having a party." Looking again at Grim, she reached out with her thumb and wiped at something above his lip.

"Well, aren't they disturbing the peace?"

"They've been doing that since they came here, kid."

"But they're so loud this time. We can call the police, can't we?"

"Mr. Travis did that. We're outside the city limits, don't forget. The police won't do anything. Besides, it seems they have a permit."

Her tone was flat and instructional, like someone stating the rules of a standardized test. Yet Grim suspected she was still upset, and maybe trying too hard to control it. He didn't know if she was still mad at him, or at the Hell's Angels, or at the police, or at the neighborhood's helplessness. He had the feeling that she was daring him to say something out of line, and frustrated by her own goodwill.

"Empty the mop bucket and put it in the closet," she said.

Aunt Ruth arrived late in the afternoon, just before dusk. By that time, the music was still loud and the Hell's Angels had been whooping some. Rita had telephoned her earlier in the morning to tell her what to expect, but Aunt Ruth still looked shaken as she described how a biker carrying a liquor-guzzling girl on the back sped past her as she entered the street. Grim was surprised when Rita laughed.

When he went to get Aunt Ruth's bags from her car, Dwight and Lydell pedaled by the house and waved. Grim had forgotten about his bicycle. He knew it would still be at the basketball court whenever he went for it, but he was suddenly so disappointed that he didn't care.

At dinner, Rita and Aunt Ruth talked about the Hell's Angels, about other relatives, about Aunt Ruth's church. Grim said only what he had to for politeness, and he decided that wasn't much. He and Dwight and Lydell had been pitiful. No one in the whole adult community had been able to do anything. Grim doubted that had his own parents been there they would have done anything either. He wanted someone to show him how not to be defeated, and this defeat seemed as if it would last forever.

After dinner he went out and sat on the front porch and listened to the music and the voices through the woods. He recognized a Merle Haggard song. It was dark now, and lightning bugs swirled about in the yard. After awhile Rita and Aunt Ruth came out, holding tall glasses of vodka-and-tonic, their favorite drink when they were together. Aunt Ruth was certainly older and heavier, but they looked alike. Grim's mother had been the oldest of the girls in her family, but sometimes Aunt Ruth called Rita by his mother's name, and Rita would call Aunt Ruth "Mom." Aunt Ruth lit a cigarette from the leather case she carried and sat on the top porch step. Rita placed her hand on Grim's shoulder. "So they're having a party," she said. She looked out at the lightning bugs in the trees at the edge of the woods. "Must be some party."

"It's practically next door," Aunt Ruth said.

"Let's go see."

Aunt Ruth exhaled smoke. "Sure. Let's have a look at those Hell's Angels."

They set their drinks on the railings and started off the porch. As Aunt Ruth crushed her cigarette on the ground with her foot, Rita looked back at Grim. They were serious. Rita hadn't been in those woods in years. Aunt Ruth had probably never been in them. But Grim was the one who had thrown the rocks, and, he realized with dread, if the Hell's Angels wanted to take it out on someone, he couldn't let it be his sister and his aunt alone.

The night sky was bright enough so that they could see the path at the side of the house. Rita led and Grim was in the rear. He was already almost taller than either of them, but they weren't tall. The Hell's Angels were huge. He had never felt dumber, not even when his first-grade teacher would send him out to the hall to see what time it was before he learned to read a clock. Now he felt as if his time was up. He felt like the sacrificial boy to a god he suddenly didn't believe in. They came upon a group of people in the woods near where he, Dwight and Lydell had spied on the Hell's Angels. Some torches had been stuck in the clearing, and two of the men cradled rifles. The others were drinking beer, but no one approached.

Rita walked up to one of the rifle bearers. He had a red-tipped dagger tattooed on his shoulder. His arms seemed larger than Grim's chest.

"What are you all doing?" Rita asked. She didn't smile, but she didn't sound hostile, either.

The man looked at her without moving, with a surprisingly bemused expression. "We're having a picnic, ma'am. It's an annual event."

"You're going to do this every year?"

"That's right."

"Where do you all come from?"

"All over."

While Rita talked to the man, Aunt Ruth had her arm around Grim. Grim didn't want to be seen this way, but her arm felt good. Rita stepped over a root and looked across the road for a better view of the house. Under a string of lights, a line of picnic tables, heaped with bowls of food and tubs of beer, lined the sloping yard. People milled about and some danced to the country music. Others lounged on the sunken seats of the motorcycles.

Rita walked to where Grim and Aunt Ruth stood by the man with the rifle. A girl in fringed, buckskin boots handed the man a joint. The rifle was heavy-looking with a rich brown stock. Another man ambled by with a sheathed knife in his studded belt.

"So you're the Hell's Angels," Rita said.

"Yes, ma'am."

"I wish you'd get the hell away from here."

The man looked down at Rita and arched his eyebrows.

"Yes, sir," Aunt Ruth said. "Go party with your home-boys in hell."

The man smiled slowly, but his eyes had grown cold.

"Good evening, then," Aunt Ruth said, and she led the way back to the house. Grim thought that if he looked behind him he'd catch a bullet between his eyes. Aunt Ruth and Rita walked excruciatingly slowly. Grim focused on their pastel sweat suits and sneakers. The different colors seemed identical in the pale light and shadows on the path.

They sat on the porch steps and laughed, falling into each other. Grim stood looking at them, still scared and bewildered. Suddenly they stopped and stared above his head.

"Look at that lonesome old moon way up in the sky," they said dreamily.

Grim turned and saw the perfect white moon cresting the trees. By the way they had spoken in unison, he knew it was probably a song lyric from before he was born. He could imagine his father inside the house putting the record on the console record player, and his mother on the step singing with them.

Rita succeeded in getting rid of the Hell's Angels, thanks to a petition submitted during a neighborhood meeting. Members of the gang actually attended, invited by Rita. Sitting on pews in the church on Tate Road, the bikers concurred that although the area was rural it was nevertheless populated, and that noise from revving motorcycles and parties disturbed the neighbors' peace. They agreed that for the safety of the children and old people speed limits should be observed. And they knew the sheriff had his eye on them. After a year, they didn't renew their lease on Mr. Brown's house. Somebody else did—a quieter, transient bunch—and over time that house was one of several inhabited by unfamiliar folk.

Credentials

OVER THE YEARS, Rita's student "Belly Man" grew bigger, more confident and cooler. He was so arrogant that eventually he was sent to prison. But he got out.

He waited in the auto-tag line and checked the manila envelope again for his new driver's license, plus the insurance card and title for the Lincoln he had managed to keep. The fleet of cars for his old car-rental business was gone. But he was starting fresh, starting legal.

He had been standing forty minutes and still had twelve people in front of him. Only two of the eight windows were staffed. The line behind him curved out the door into the hallway. This was a new building, constructed when Belly Man was in prison. It was an open, marble place with tall leafy trees growing in the wide lobby. As the man directly behind him was saying, they had all this beautiful marble and shit and no clerks to sell the licenses. The man was talking to a buddy. They were young, and from what Belly overheard, they worked in a nightclub as bartenders or bouncers, maybe one of each. They wore stiff, baggy brown and black denim clothes and heavy shoes. They had high-and-tight haircuts, and one wore oval lens, black-wire glasses. With their thick necks they looked like the young inmates who sweated out their time in the weight room.

Their talk was mostly about people who came to the club. Everybody had a nickname.

"Asphalt hitting on Rooster's wife."

"Yeah, but she too old."

"You see me put him out the other night? For his own good."

"Clock tried to sneak in. He still hasn't grown up."

"Clock? Pig's brother?"

"Yeah. I hadn't seen Clock since last summer on Smiley Street. Clock was so happy he wanted to wrestle. We were bumping our heads against curbs under cars until the police rolled up."

"You going to Skate's cookout?"

"Don't eat meat anymore; you know that."

"Since when?"

"Since Tuney. She won't let me. Man, she won't buy a package of bread without reading the ingredients.

Like what's new in bread? That woman lives too right."

"Yeah, well, how you living? You can't eat no more ribs."

"That's all right. Your girl likes it when my mouth ain't greasy."

Belly Man chuckled. The men went on talking about people named Goosebump, Streetlight, Chaos and Brick.

But Belly Man was patient. He had learned patience while spending a year and a half of a five-year sentence. Manslaughter. An accident, really, but a violent one. It had been his fault. He knew that now. Quick temper. But he had learned to count to ten, as they say, count to whatever it took. With good behavior, he hadn't had to count five years.

His credentials bore his real name, Byron Isaac Mason. In prison he had been either Mason or his number. Early on, he told the cons to call him Ike, but that didn't stick. Just a week before he was paroled, a guy who knew him came on the block calling him Belly Man. In no time the rest of the crowd picked it up, even the guards. He had a big gut. So what? He was proud of being big. He liked a big car and he liked a big reputation. But changing his life might be hard. He couldn't even change his name.

Belly thought about people he knew but hadn't seen in awhile. He'd been on parole for the last year, laying real low, watching cartoons, working two jobs at the mental hospital—in the kitchen by day and mopping halls by night. Thankfully, he'd come across none of his acquaintances at the hospital—he'd expected at least a couple of drug rehabs—and he could never think of anyone he really wanted to see from the old days. Safer that way;

judge's orders, even. The only straight-up guy he thought about now and then was Grim Power, who had dumped his moronic street rodeo act, it seemed, and now was towing cars. He wondered what Grim's real name was.

Belly Man had seen Grim hitching up a van in the hospital parking lot, actually the drop-off lane at the front door. A kid had come barreling up one night to commit himself and plowed into the back of a car that had gotten there first. Nobody was hurt, but the police came, and then Grim in the tow truck with "Power" professionally painted on the door. Maybe, Belly Man thought, he'd check out Grim now that he was through with parole, now that he had saved some money and was ready to make a deal.

Two weeks later on a Saturday, Belly Man had another afternoon off. He decided to go downtown to his old barbershop for a haircut and shave. Since he'd been out, he'd been cutting his hair himself using scissors and two mirrors. His head usually looked it, crooked and plucked, though he had gotten better. But he'd decided that he was coming back—Belly Man but different, gentler. He wanted his own business again; he didn't know what kind, and getting groomed seemed a good first step. People needed to know he was back; he needed to know what people were doing.

He dressed in his trademark burgundy clothes, including a short-brimmed straw cap, and parked around the corner from the shop. He hesitated before coming to the shop window, and walked away angry at himself toward the downtown park, trying to pump up his purpose.

The park was a medium-size circle of grass and trees

for office workers and vagrants. Belly Man sat on a bench bordering one of the narrow, paved paths and looked at the oak and magnolia trees in the short distance. He thought people were sitting up in the trees but, his mind clearing, he saw that sheets and blankets were stuffed in the crook of the branches, the bedding of the vagrants and homeless. He thought of the Lost Boys of the Peter Pan story. He scanned the park and noticed a city maintenance man picking up trash around a stone water fountain.

The man wore a drab green shirt and pants. He pulled a trash barrel on wheels. As he got closer he became the best-looking trash man Belly Man had seen—neat thick hair shot with gray, matching well-groomed beard, shirt-tail in, absorbed in his work, self-motivated. He looked like somebody famous, a singer. Belly Man could picture him working in his new business, whatever it might be, attractive, hardworking, a good guy for customers to see, a moneymaker.

"Minute by Minute," Belly Man called out. "You look just like that Doobie Brother, man. Anybody ever tell you that?"

The man glanced up but went back to work.

In prison a lot of guys looked like somebody else. On the yard Belly Man wiled away a lot of time making those connections. One guy looked like a short, strung-out Abra-ham Lincoln—moustacheless beard, hollow cheeks, rock-edge bones; and another had the soft, scruffy face of Yassar Arafat. The con that ran the library did everything he could to look like Malcolm X, only he didn't have red hair. Belly Man's barber inside was a dead ringer for Levi Stubbs of The Four Tops. For a month Belly was afraid he *was* Levi Stubbs, until he found out the guy had done twelve years of a life sentence for kidnaping and murder, and Belly thought he would have known if Levi had been locked down in this state for that crime. A lot of those look-alikes were in for murder, though Abraham Lincoln and Yassar Arafat claimed innocence. All the murderers and manslaughterers were known as "The Deadly Killers." The drug dealers and counterfeiters called them that.

The park janitor got close enough. "I know you're not deaf. Look, I'm trying to get something together. You might want to get in on it."

The guy kept silent, spearing paper cups and burger wrappers. Belly Man figured what the hell. He might recruit this guy to work for him, or he might not. He said, "It's true, I did kill somebody and I was incarcerated. But I'm a good boss. I mean"—he chuckled—"the guy I killed didn't work for me." Belly Man watched the man struggle to spear a cigarette butt. Finally, the man bent to pick it up. "We got in a shoving match, he tripped on something, hit his head."

The guy examined the nail on his stick, licked the tip.

"I guess you like the job you already got. Work at your own pace, outdoors, fresh air, nobody telling you to hurry up."

"Look, *you* like this job? Let *me* sit on a bench all day. These squirrels are sneaky, and somebody out here is killing pigeons and I have to clean that up." He didn't look like anybody when he talked. His mouth went sloppy and loose. "I have a chemical imbalance, dammit, but they expect me to come to work everyday. Got the *nerve* to ask me why I'm late sometime. Hell, the medicine alone will

mess you up, the son of a *bitches*. They don't understand
nothing; you can't get along with them; the supervisor he
don't want to listen, and he expects me to pay attention.
I'm *sick*, dammit, and I have *shown* them my papers."

He stabbed the ground while he ranted. Belly Man got
up, hiked up his pants, and began walking back to the
barbershop. Not all handsome white guys would be good
employees, he decided. He knew he should have known;
his cellmate at the city jail before he was transferred to
state prison was an arsonist who had Paul Newman's eyes
and swagger.

A half block up, Belly Man looked back and somehow
the park guy had gotten all the way down under the
blanket-crammed oaks. He must have run. Maybe his
chemical imbalance gave him super speed. Belly wondered
where the keepers of the bundles in the trees were, probably on street corners holding hand-scrawled signs begging
for food money. He could have been one of them. There
came a time in prison when, if he could have gotten a
gallon jug of wine to cradle against a Dumpster in an
alley everyday, he would have gratefully drunk himself to
death.

But those months passed. He still had a house, though
his little sister and Dot, his ex-girlfriend, had sold most of
the furniture and kept the money. At least he had sold
his rental inventory himself, mostly to Grim Power, for
legal bills. He had stocked only a couple of minivans, two
Cadillac limos, and four Corollas he had bought from
Hertz, and a backhoe.

Grim had bought the Corollas, a van and the backhoe.
Belly guessed that he turned around and sold them for

profit, probably how he had managed to get the big pretty tow truck. Grim was one of the few to visit him in prison, but like the others had dropped off after the first year. Belly didn't mind; he wouldn't have visited anybody either.

Bells jingled with his entry into the barbershop. His barber still had the first chair. Ed wore a black barber's smock and a white mask over his mouth and nose as he worked. He was allergic to hair. He pulled down the mask and grinned when he saw Belly Man standing in the door.

"I don't believe anything, anymore," Ed said. "You're back."

"Who asked you?"

"I'm glad. But, uh-ruh-huh, things are different around here. You need an appointment now."

Belly Man glanced around. The other three barbers were busy cutting hair. They were younger guys he didn't recognize. Instead of smocks they wore linen shorts and silk print shirts. Five or six other young men waited, reading magazines or looking up at a television mounted in the corner over Belly Man's head.

"I need what?"

"You don't really need one, you know. We encourage them, that's all. Hold up." Ed switched off the clippers he was using to trim his customer's neck and consulted his appointment book. "I can sign you in now. You can be next."

"Shit. I guess *you* need some appointments."

"Appointments don't do you no good," the man in the chair said. He had a white goatee. His black shoes were glossed, and his black socks were ribbed and see-through, the style Belly Man wore. "I been waiting a hour for one of those boys down there, and finally had to let old Ed take over. I got to get back to work."

"Old Ed, my butt."

"That's *Mr.* Ed," said the barber at the next chair. "Say it with respect."

"That's a talking horse, Chief," Ed said.

Belly Man sat under a framed pencil-drawing of a teary-eyed boy having his hair cut by a kindly old man. Other pictures on the wall showed barber scenes, too— barbers tending to their customers draped in white, hair on the floor, men in suits and ties waiting their turns. Before, all Ed had up were photos of heads modeling different haircuts, which a guy was supposed to come in and point to as the one he'd like. But as far as Belly could remember, nobody ever asked for one of those prissy v-neck or pompadour styles. Ed always cut people's hair to look just like his, a little full on top and combed back, narrow on the sides, fading out in the back at the neck.

The television showed a movie about a town invaded by giant rabbits, and every few seconds Ed would glance up at it, neglecting the job he was doing. "Uh-ruh, wonder what would happen if those big rabbits came here." The screen showed a terrified woman hiding under a coffee table while a rabbit's eye filled her window.

"I'd get my shotgun and kick some rabbit ass," shouted a man sitting near Belly Man.

"Them rabbits there are on drugs. That's how they got like that. To them, we'd look like a bunch of wild carrots running around."

"I bet the National Guard would get rolling. There'd be tanks and rabbits squaring off on the highways."

"I know one thing," said one of the customers on the other side of Belly Man. "I'd steal me a Jaguar and get the hell out of here. I'd steal *two* Jags, one for me and one for Gladys Knight, who I'd save from rabbit fury and then marry."

"There won't be no giant rabbits coming here. So don't worry about it."

"I know that, Belly Man. But what if?"

"Damn," Belly Man said. He picked up a magazine from a chair next to him. Every page was of a black woman in a swimsuit. He looked back at the cover but it was half torn away, the magazine's title missing.

A man wearing a red-white-and-gray leather cycle-racing suit and carrying a matching helmet came in the door.

"Welcome!" Ed said.

"That's right. Thank you very much."

"You're Welcome."

"Everyday, all the time."

The other barbers laughed. One said, "It's a good thing your name's not Good-bye. You'd always be leaving."

"A good-bye is what I hope to eschew."

"Gesundheit," Belly Man said.

The man looked over at Belly. He laughed. "Thanks."

Everybody shouted, "You're Welcome!"

Mr. Welcome stood wide-legged, his hands on his hips under his short, zipped jacket. "I'm up next, right, Ed?"

"Uh-ruh, not unless you got an appointment."

"I have one."

"What time?"

"Well, this current time right here, Ed. Don't you know your own schedule?"

"I got somebody ahead of you," pointing his clippers at Belly Man.

"Oh, yeah?" He took off his leather jacket, revealing a red T-shirt. He didn't seem to need either a haircut or a shave. Belly figured he was one of those guys who couldn't let himself get that far. "Maybe we can work something out," the man said. He sat beside Belly Man in the chair where the swimsuit book had been, and hung the jacket casually over the chairback. He placed his helmet on the floor by his feet. His boots were of the same colorful leather as his pants and jacket.

"You must have a pretty good lead to have time to stop for a haircut," Belly Man said.

"Oh." The man laughed. "I wear this when I ride lately. Some other guys and I are in a club. The fact is I'm in pretty much of a hurry. How about letting me go first. Ed's always messing up this appointment business. I swear to you I called for this half-hour, too."

"I can't think you'd lie for a haircut. But we used to have a rule about first-come, first-serve. And if that ain't good enough no more, then my name is on Ed's book where yours ain't."

"My name is Lonnie, by the way. What's yours?"

Belly Man shook the man's hand and considered what name to give. "It's Byron Belly Man Mason."

"Duh-uh-ruh," said Ed, "Bryon?"

"Belly Man? What are you, a wrestler?" Lonnie asked.

"No."

"O.K. But you're famous, aren't you? I heard that name somewhere."

"You ever been at state prison?"

"I've been by there. But that's not where I know the

name. You an inmate, or you work there? Are you on
work release?"

"We on a game show here?"

"I know something about, you know, law and crime.
So I don't want to presume, but you must have done some
time recently. I must have read about you. I used to work
in the D.A.'s office but now I'm for the defense." Lonnie
reached back for his jacket and pulled a business card
from the pocket.

Belly Man took it, scissored it between two fingers. "So
you for the people now. Thanks, but I'm without those
troubles for a while. Where were you three years ago?
Probably writing up arguments to send me away."

"What are you into these days? Got anything going?
It's usually rough just getting out. You on parole?"

Belly Man didn't respond. He frowned at Ed as if to
say, Who is this guy? Ed finished brushing the loose hair
off his customer's shoulders and let the man up. "Lonnie,
Belly Man used to have the only black-owned car-rental
business in town. He's a businessman."

Lonnie crossed one leather leg over the other leather
knee. "Me, too. I got a few investments besides my law
practice, which is part-time now anyway. My first love is
art, though. Drawing. I'm in art school. But still there's
Thompson's Lawn Care, Cockman's Cleaners. I do a little
with Power Towing—you know Grim Power?"

Belly Man nodded. He knew all of them.

"I've been thinking about the food business lately.
You'd look good as a restaurant man yourself. Belly Man's
Barbecue, maybe. Of course, you'd eat all the inventory,
wouldn't you?"

Ed laughed as he swept out the seat of the barber chair.

Belly Man took a deep breath and started counting to ten. He went on to twelve and then got up. "Too bad you ain't got no barbershop. Maybe then you could get waited on." He stepped over and sat down in the chair.

"You'd think so, wouldn't you?" Lonnie looked at Ed, mildly disgusted.

"Ah, shit. You got a piece of this place, too. I bet this appointment stuff was your idea, wasn't it?" He climbed down and with a wave of his arm presented the chair to Lonnie. "You go ahead then, boss man. I ain't in a hurry."

"Thanks. I really have to get somewhere."

Ed shook out the barber's cape and floated it down around Lonnie. He fastened it around Lonnie's neck and busied himself at the counter behind the chair, sorting through combs and clipper guards.

"You know what I thought you were when you walked in here in that outfit? A Power Ranger."

Everybody in the shop laughed. Lonnie replied, "O.K. That's good."

"That's right on time," said the barber down at the last chair. "I used to see them Power Rangers every day on TV. I knew Lonnie reminded me of something."

"Yeah," Belly said, "I bet Lonnie's got the videos."

"Hey, I've been trying to get Grim to join the bike club like me and Ed," Lonnie said. "We could change our name to the Rangers, and Grim really *would* be a Power Ranger."

"Uh-huh. That would be stupid, too."

Ed pumped up the chair. "I can do you in an hour, Belly. For real. There's a guy due in right after Lonnie, but after that I just got you." He went to work combing and cutting Lonnie's hair.

Lonnie said. "You give me a call if you get any ideas."

Belly returned to looking at the magazine full of swimsuit models. He had some ideas. One thing he'd noticed since he got out was the opening of black stripper clubs. He'd been to one, all the girls plain naked. He was thinking about getting into that, getting some young good-looking girls like in that book. He was also thinking about a janitorial service. He'd planned to talk with Grim about it, but maybe this Lonnie guy would be his man.

The back barber, in a shirt with large green flowers, began talking about the death of Dinah Shore. He was shocked, just shocked and saddened, he said. because he'd just seen her on A & E the week before. She was so talented and so courageous. And it was strange how so many musicians were blind, and he wanted to know if everybody knew she was black.

"She sounded black," one of the barbers said.

"I didn't know she was blind."

"I didn't know she was dead."

"That woman's not dead," one of the guys waiting said. "She'll be in concert at the civic center next week."

"She is, too, dead. She's *been* dead. It was on the news."

Belly Man stood up. "Goddamn gracious. Y'all have got everything all mixed up. The one that's dead is dead. The one that's blind is not. Neither one of them is black." He headed for the door. "I been in prison and I know more than you busters."

As he went out, he heard Ed explaining things to the other barbers; Dinah Shore was dead; Dianne Shurr was not. Good, Belly Man thought, somebody's got some sense, even if it's Ed.

He strolled past shops on the street and tried out names for his new business. He had called the car-rental venture Belly Man's Rentals. But now, for the strip joint, he considered Mason's Minxes, and Belly's Browns. For the maintenance service he thought of using his full name: Byron Mason's Maintenance. Or B.M.'s Janitorial Service. His initials were as bad as they could be. He'd always hated his name, and he didn't much like his nickname. But he'd have to use Belly Man because he wanted no mistakes. He wanted people to know who he was, to know he was back, even if he had to cozy up to these young money guys to get there.

There was a time when the youngsters were afraid of him. In prison most people seemed afraid of nothing, especially the ones who had been there awhile. Belly had been afraid the whole time. Afraid he'd never get out, afraid he'd forget about who he was. During the year of parole, at night mopping halls, he often wished he had forgotten more. He sometimes thought he should have stayed in longer, to be as thoroughly stripped as the others. They had gotten new hard-core selves inside—the Muslims, orthodox and otherwise; the Jews; white-supremacists; rapists; Christians; Buddhists; lawyers; revolutionaries. They had gone past the fear of losing themselves and seemed to latch firmly onto deep faith in a self they really always wanted, rotten or not. So Belly Man sometimes regretted not going that far. He wondered now if he was anything like those people in the mental hospital where he worked, at least the ones who knew where they were; he didn't expect to get back the person he had been, but he hadn't lost enough to be someone new.

As for his new business, he wouldn't let that Lonnie name it. Anybody who rode around town in a Power Ranger suit was used to getting his way, but Belly was used to getting his way, too. And he wasn't about to put on a tight leather suit and ride around with a bunch of pretty boys on motorcycles just to get this guy's investment. He imagined, though, cruising along over bridges. He saw himself thinner, hunched over the handlebars and whisking into the wind. Finally, he saw himself alone, leaving the pack behind. He couldn't hook onto any group, no matter who he was, not like those prisoners who identified with any old ready-made mass entity. Hell—he chuckled—he was a mass entity unto himself.

He had a notion to drive around, maybe swing by Grim's and a few other old places. Maybe make some appointments. He liked the idea of having his own scheduled time to get his haircut. That was a progressive improvement, suitable to the convenience he would prefer for his next lifestyle. But, no, he wouldn't be caught thrumming through the streets with a bunch of leather boys. Besides, he thought, rounding the corner toward his big burgundy car, he was a Lincoln man, built for comfort, always would be.

Damaged Luxury

RITA MARRIED HER boyfriend Mayes. She put her house in the care of a property manager and moved out of town, first to Louisiana, where Mayes became a physicist, and later to other cities—wherever his jobs and research took him. She believed he was brilliant. When Grim dropped out of college and stopped visiting them wherever they happened to live, she gave him the house. There were years of adventures, with Rita acquiring new children to rear and Grim acquiring new identities. He meditated at a monastery, raced cars in Nevada, became a show-business cowboy. He came home, went away, and eventually moved back to stay—brought his horse with him. He rode in parades, sometimes the horse and sometimes old cars, which he bought and restored and sold. He made his living with cars. He loved them. He bought them, sold them, fixed them, and towed them. It was during one particular transaction that he fell in love with a woman. And she fell for him. Though neither could gauge the depth.

At eight on an August Monday morning, the woman, Phyllis Clark—called Butter by her boyfriend Grim, and by most every other adult she knew in town—brought her Corvette to be polished at Belly Man's Exchequer Car Wash and Detail Shop. Belly Man had been trying to swing a deal to wash all of Grim's tow trucks and used cars, so as a favor he loaned her a teal Electra 225. The car had a black fake convertible top and gleaming gold chrome trim. A strip of gold mirror bearing the words "Layin' Low" in hologram ran along the bottom side panels from front wheel to back.

It was a hard car to drive. The exhaust thundered, the ceiling fabric sagged and the signal lights didn't work. The electric seats moved backward only. Butter wondered whether or not the brake lights worked, whether or not the car would bring the police down on her. Belly Man's reputation meant there was no telling how he had gotten the car, or what crime it might have been used for. It practically screamed, "Search me." If Grim could see her now, he'd either laugh or demand she get out of the car immediately. She couldn't decide which would please her more. She had met him almost a year ago, when she hit town and was looking for a used car. He fed her grilled fish and sold her the Corvette, saying it fit her, saying it was freedom formed of fiberglass. He made himself irresistible. Now, he seemed pretty much family.

She was on her way to Sacred Lamb School, where she taught first grade. Classes wouldn't start for three weeks but she wanted to hang posters of clever-looking animals representing the alphabet, and to have a look at some of the new children who would be there to take diagnostic tests. Besides, she had been spending too much time with Grim and his cronies—filling in as tow-truck dispatcher and playing hostess at Grim's parties.

She eased into the school's neighborhood of old houses, on a block of brick side streets. She had to wait behind a cream-colored station wagon at a stop sign where a barefoot man was leaning into the driver's window. The man was bearded and animated. He smiled big, and Butter began to doubt he was begging; maybe he and the woman behind the wheel knew each other. It was a sweet idea— delight shared across socioeconomic classes like that. A little girl's bright red pigtails popped into view in the backseat. Finally the car moved and the man waved goodbye.

As Butter rolled to the stop sign, the man stayed in the road and waved. His beard was thick and gray, his skin glistening and dark. His smile was beautiful, Butter thought. Where'd he get those teeth? He bent to her window and said, "Give me a goddamn, motherfucking quarter."

Butter laughed. "You want a quarter? I might have a quarter." She looked in her purse. "All I have is a son-of-a-bitch dollar."

"Give it to me, baby. You want my shirt? I already gave away my shoes. I'm just out here, doing *nothing* wrong."

"Sure. I believe that."

"Everything I do is right." He began to recite the Pledge of Allegiance while Butter found some change in the bottom of her purse and handed it to him with the dollar.

"Enjoy these shit-faced dimes, too," she said, interrupting him.

The man reared back in laughter. "I ain't *got* nothing else." She watched him in her rearview mirror as she drove away. He was hopping up and down laughing. His happiness must have scared that other woman and little girl to death, she thought. They hadn't given him any money.

She maneuvered the Buick into a faculty space on the school lot. Children and parents were getting out of station wagons and minivans in the paved courtyard, and a girl new to Butter came over to her. "Hi."

"Nice ride," said the girl. She looked to be about nine years old, fourth grade. She wore a dress, blue with white rosebuds. Her feet, in brand-new cross trainers, looked oversized.

"I borrowed it." She squeezed the sore muscle at the nape of her neck and wagged her head. "It's painful."

"I can drive," the girl said, scanning the car. "My dad lets me."

"Really? Are you going to be a student here?"

"Me and my sister—the one just under me, not my two baby sisters, because they're just babies. You're a teacher, I guess. Why don't you have your own car?"

"I do." She reached for the posters in the backseat.

Loose tobacco lined the creases of the tight leather uphol-
stery. "It's a Corvette. Can you drive a Corvette?"

"My sister's name is Corvette. All of us are named for
Chevy's, because my daddy likes them so much. Beretta
and Lumina are the babies. I'm Camaro. So of course I
can drive a 'Vette." She smirked.

"Well, all right. That's all right. Where are you supposed to be now?"

"In there." She pointed to the school office. "I gotta
show these new Sisters how smart I am. I always make
A's. Nobody can believe me. You won't either. Don't you
want to know my last name?"

"O.K."

"M-e-l-l-o. Mello."

"I'm Miss Clark." She decided not to spell it. "First
grade."

"I'm way past that. You might get my sister though."

"I wouldn't be surprised."

"This is a sharp car. It's loaded, isn't it? What's it got?
Remote entry? Turbo? After-factory specials? Automatic
inside and out?"

Butter looked at the car and noticed for the first time
the thin, gold ribbony swirls under the gold door handles.
With its teal-tinted windows and gold hubcaps it looked
like something won at the fair. "What doesn't it have?"

They went to the school together. Parents and children
filled the office and the small chairs set up in the hallways.

"There's my mom. See you." She bounced over to a
woman who didn't look like she would allow her children
to be named for cars.

Half an hour later Butter had hung her posters and

organized the materials she would use in her classroom. First graders were lining up in the hallway beside Sister Eunice, the vice principal, about to lead them into the media room for the exam. This was what Butter had wanted to see, the gathering of sweet-faced children still small and soft, before they hardened into individual personalities and Butter hardened into teacher.

She tried to pick out Camaro's sister. There were only four black children in the line of a dozen. All four were girls. The one that most resembled Camaro had a head full of thick braids and colorful translucent barrettes. And then Camaro's mother went over to straighten the child's elastic-waist skirt. When Sister Eunice led the first graders away, Butter decided to introduce herself. Camaro was already saying, "Mom, that's Miss Clark."

"I see Camaro has told you about me. She's some super girl. I wanted to meet you, because I might have your other daughter in class this year."

"Then you'll have your hands full," Mrs. Mello said. "These girls are too excited about coming here. They love school."

"So do I."

"If I were six years old and you were my teacher, I'd be ecstatic. You look so with it, with the earrings and the pretty short hair." She smiled approvingly. "And your complexion is so wonderfully dark and clean. You're beautiful."

Butter blushed and touched the earrings. They were an abstract arrangement of triangles she had bought at the art museum. She let her fingers feel along her face. "Thank you." She could handle a compliment.

"We just moved here from the most well-behaved town on the planet, in Alabama. I learned to acquire nondisturbing possessions just to live peacefully there. We're lucky my husband is a physicist and keeps getting better jobs. It's so liberating. We only lived there three years. We're a restless family." She laughed. She sat with terrific posture, knees together, hands in her lap. She wore crisp lime-green pants and blouse—some kind of linen blend —and her longish curled hair had a gray patch at the widow's peak. She looked a little older than Grim, who was forty. She would be Grim's type if he went for women anywhere near his own age.

"Mrs. Mello, did you go to charm school?"

She reached to touch Butter's hand. "Don't flatter me," she whispered. "I was trained to be a teacher myself. I last taught in a Louisiana swamp and it scared the poise out of me. I wasn't trained for that, let me tell you." She laughed again.

"Tell about the boy," Camaro said.

"Oh, a boy attacked me with a lawn-mower blade. He hacked the chalkboard to pieces and set the whole class to screaming. I escaped by hiding under my desk to compose my resignation letter."

"My mom is so cool."

"Well, that's a requirement. Where else have you lived?"

"Arizona, California, Massachusetts. Camaro was born there. Corvette is my California girl. It's a wonder we didn't name her Malibu."

"I lived in Philadelphia," Butter found herself saying. There was something intimate about knowing the names of this woman's children, and she felt compelled to give something of herself. "I was called Philly Pie by everybody all through high school, and then my parents divorced and my mother began calling me Phyllis. I think it was part of her plan to get more distance from Dad. That was tough, but *I* escaped when they sent me to a Minnesota college, where I was just plain Phyllis universally. And now I'm Butter, by the way, which was my point."

"Good. I'm better, too."

"No, I'm sorry. I mean that I'm called Butter."

"Why?"

"My boyfriend started it." No need to tell her *his* name. "I think it's a Southern thing. Something about my skin, he says."

"Oh, oh, oh," Mrs. Mello rolled her eyes.

"What?" Camaro asked. "He likes butter a whole lot."

"I guess so." She looked at the book Camaro was holding, an outdated third-grade reader she must have gotten from the counter in the office. It had a silvery cover of a raccoon in a rowboat and it highlighted the girl's innocence, making Butter feel both young and mature at the same time. This feeling was precisely why she loved the company of Grim, who was seventeen years her senior. She let the satisfaction of having figured all this out shimmer through her.

"Anyway, this is a great school," she said. "No lawn-tool crimes."

"It's why we chose it, exactly. This is my home, you see. My husband's, too. The children have never even visited though. Never met their uncle—my brother—or my husband's family. They're all adopted, you should know, all our daughters. We thought it about time we came back, to let them know who we might be. Who they might be."

Camaro stood up, spun around, and sat back down. "Let's go get something to eat."

"Honey, you've already had breakfast," Mrs. Mello said.

"Yeah, but that wore off. There's a whole hour before they call me."

Mrs. Mello looked at her watch. "But we have to be here when Corvette comes out." Mrs. Mello turned to Butter. "Is there a snack machine in the school?"

"I'm afraid not." Strange children and parents were making friends all up and down the hall. The school librarian hustled by and nodded to her.

"This is your home? Really?" Butter asked.

"I'm afraid so. We've been trying to get back. We finally got the opportunity."

"Wait a minute. Forgive me, but this is faintly familiar. Does your brother know you're here?"

Mrs. Mello stared at Butter a moment, seemed to look at her earrings and eyes, a serene smile on her face. "We spoke last night. I'm sorry." She laid her fingers on Butter's knee. "He told me about you. But when you mentioned your boyfriend, I realized he hadn't told you. And now I'm embarrassed for us all."

"You're Rita, then?"

She nodded.

"You know my uncle?" Camaro asked. "*He's* your boyfriend?"

"I don't understand."

"You'll have to ask him, I'm afraid. He has known we were coming, but not exactly when. The girls and I drove in yesterday to enroll in school. My husband will follow next week."

"Was he trying to surprise me?" Butter asked.

"He always *liked* surprises. And jokes. I did think you knew. It seemed so rightly serendipitous that you and Camaro had met. I believed that all was very perfect."

"Well, apparently all is—a little."

"Don't be frightened. Grim and I have been estranged, that's all. Amicably, but still we haven't been very close. He probably hasn't yet made room for us in his day-to-day thoughts. It shouldn't mean that he doesn't love you. Or me, for that matter."

"He talked about you when we first met. That you raised him and adopted some kids." She glanced at Camaro, who was sitting slumped and sullen, as if mad that her uncle Grim had discovered Butter before she did. "You know, I don't know how to feel right now," Butter continued. "I'm angry but very pleased, too. Your being here is an odd secret for him to keep."

"Maybe he's selfish," Rita said.

"No, he's not."

"Why can't we eat?" Camaro asked.

"We're foodless," Rita said. "That's why."

Camaro bared her teeth at her mother, kid-fierce.

"I know a place about seven minutes from here," Butter said. "I'll take you. I'm hungry, too."

Camaro jutted out her neck and widened her eyes at her mother, pleading. Rita adjusted the blue bow on Camaro's hair and regarded Butter again. "I'd better stay. Take the munchkin."

"Yes!"

"Oh, no," Butter said. "You have to come, too. There's a rule, I think. Anyway, I'd prefer it."

"A rule? Really?"

Butter looked at Camaro. "It was a bad idea. You know about rules."

"Come on, Mom."

"Let's put it this way. You have my permission. It's perfectly all right. You'll bring me something back." She pulled some money from her purse and gave it to Camaro.

Camaro crushed the dollars in her fist. "Be good," she said to her mother.

"What's this place we're going to?" Camaro sat low beside Butter in the car, the safety belt grazing her chin.

"It's a bagel shop. You can get sandwiches and salads, too. Chips." She wished she had time to take Camaro to meet Grim, but that was outside the city limits. He would appreciate Camaro, the whole Chevrolet family—which was his, remarkably—and the beautiful, profane beggar, too. She hadn't met people this entertaining until she started hanging out with Grim. Belly Man, the paroled car-wash entrepeneur, whose office door had a "Gangsters Only" sign; Dr. East, the filthy chemist who came around collecting aluminum cans in a ragged El Camino—curious people were always coming through Grim's house on business or to play. She had wanted to think that now she was meeting them on her own. She suspected Grim had set her up, or was there some other reason he hadn't told her his sister would be enrolling her children at Sacred Lamb. He might have warned her, or enticed her. It *had* to be his grand joke. Otherwise it was too creepy. Or he simply imagined it was none of her business.

Camaro fiddled with the radio and surprised Butter with the discovery of a CD player in the dashboard. She pushed buttons until Howlin' Wolf started rattling from the split speakers. Grim had the same music on cassette and played it at happy high volume at his house anytime no one complained. Camaro toyed with the digital climate-control awhile, and reset the clock to the right time. The odometer, Butter noticed, was stuck on eighty-three thousand miles. Camaro opened the glove compartment and pulled out a gun.

"Whoa, put that back."

Camaro turned it over in her hand. "It could be a pellet gun. My old neighbor had one kinda like it." She put it back in the compartment but left the door open. "Looks like a Luger, though."

Butter looked from the road to the gun to Camaro. She pulled over, shut off the engine, and used the key to lock the glove compartment.

"Do you know about guns?"

"You?"

"Why would that fool leave that thing in the car?"

"What fool?"

"Never mind." She didn't look forward to explaining this to Rita, nor to the school principal. Camaro would never keep it quiet. There would be Belly Man to explain, and a reaction from Grim of a kind she couldn't right now guess. Nothing good.

She drove onto the interstate and got off at the second exit, a gentrified area of bungalows with beveled windows and wide porches. A few blocks along was a small business section, including the blue-shingled minimall. It had a lush, narrow lawn backed by deep-orange flowers, a grocery, video store, pet shop, florist. Butter lurched to a stop beside a Previa van in front of the little bagel restaurant.

Purple bougainvillea spilled from baskets hanging outside. Butter liked to stop here on school mornings for a serene moment between a loud night at Grim's—tow trucks, police scanner, stereo, and odd characters blaring —and a day with the six-year-olds. Camaro was already out of the car, examining its gold grille and asking how to open the hood. They might as well be at Grim's, Butter thought—two car-crazy girls with a gun.

The bagel shop was staffed by the owners, a fiftyish woman and her son. The woman wore white overalls and a black derby. She asked where Butter had been hiding. The son wore gray shorts and a yellow plaid shirt, and listened to Camaro read all the labels on the Lucite bins of bagels. Butter ordered coffee and a toasted wheat bagel with vegetable spread, Camaro cinnamon-raisin and cream cheese.

No one else was in the shop, but several tables still needed to be bussed. They sat at Butter's favorite table by the window, in soft salmon-colored chairs. There were oil-on-canvas paintings, royal blue and emerald green surfacing from spaces of black, bright as illuminated glass. Camaro took a long time chewing, shifting her bagel from one hand to the other to lick cream cheese from her fingers. "Tricky," she said. When she went to wash her hands Butter told her to also clean her face. Butter pushed her own plate away, but accepted a refill of coffee when the bowler-hatted woman came around with a fresh pot.

A silver Lexus sports coupe pulled up beside the teal

Electra. Lonnie Welcome. He was wearing mirror-lens sunglasses. Recently he had been stopping by Grim's and at Grim's drink-house haunts, on a Harley that Grim coveted and Butter was afraid he'd buy. She joked with Grim that all he needed to hold on to his youth was her. A motorcycle would push his wildness over the line.

When Lonnie went to the counter, the woman took off her derby and plopped it onto his head, and he thumped its crown and bowed before giving it back. Butter was glad to be needing to leave soon. He turned with his tray and smiled in her direction He wore loose jeans, a blousy white shirt, and a wide silver bracelet on each wrist. When he got to her table he said, "Look at that, Buttercup. You got the same thing I did." He set down his tray and put his glasses in his shirt pocket. His eyes shone with ambiguous delight.

"You got the same thing, *I* did, Lonnie. Don't call me 'Buttercup.' "

"I'll just sit here with you if you don't mind."

"I'm with someone, but O.K. We're leaving in few."

"Hey, you're not here looking for me are you?"

"Of course not. Were you looking for me?"

"You're the woman a man searches for all his life. But I came for this veggie spread. I live right around the corner. I'm on my daily schedule."

"I was kidding, Lonnie, as I'm sure you were."

"What about? Really, I thought maybe Grim sent you to buy my bike. You live out there with him, don't you?"

"Not with him. Near him."

Camaro came back and stood at Butter's side. She cupped her hand over Butter's ear and whispered, "Who's this?"

Butter put her arm around Camaro and introduced her to Lonnie. But she did not tell him she was Grim's niece. "You look like an artist," Camaro said. "Did you paint these pictures in here?"

"No, I didn't." He looked harmless when he smiled. His skin and teeth seemed flawless. "But I am indeed an artist, sort of."

Butter explained why they had to leave soon, about needing to get back to school.

"You mean you two just met?" Lonnie asked. "Women are really great." When he bit into the bagel he made a face of exaggerated pleasure. "And you, Miss Butter, are a sanctified woman, like the song says. That's what we like about you."

"Who are 'we' and what song?" Butter asked.

"All the guys and dolls are we. And I'm talking about that old Marvin Gaye song."

" 'Heard It Through the Grapevine'?" Camaro asked.

"No," he said, chuckling.

" 'Ain't No Mountain High Enough'?"

"No. It's called 'Sanctified Woman.' You're a 'good girl,' like Marvin sings about. You like the clergy, I'll bet. You teach the Catholic children and everything."

"They're not all Catholic."

"I'm not," Camaro said.

"I went to that school myself," he said. "I'll bet we all have a lot in common."

"What's with those bracelets, Mr. Welcome. They soak up arthritis or something?" Camaro asked.

He extended his arm. His fingernails were buffed. "Copper does that. I'm just into silver."

"So that's your ride out there? The Car of the Year?"

He grinned. "One year. I recognize that Electra beside it. It's Belly Man's loaner, right?"

"Belly what?" Camaro made a cute, skeptical face. "Can I have a peek?" She looked to Butter for approval. Butter told her to ask Lonnie, and he nodded.

"Just stay where I can see you," Butter said. "Don't touch anything. Watch out for cars."

Camaro laughed. "Right." She went out the door.

"It's hard to avoid having things in common," Butter said, gazing after Camaro.

"Thank the Lord. You know, I have a sister about that girl's age."

"Yeah? You can lay off the religion talk. I don't teach religion."

"It's O.K. to like me, Butter. Grim and I are friends."

"Like, are you a drug dealer or what? Everybody else is at work."

"I'm serious about my admiration of you. You got me stereotyped."

"I just met the proudest homeless guy on the planet, probably, and Camaro out there is from a brilliant family named for Chevrolets. All of that is quite beautiful and sad to me. You, on the other hand, are not so original."

"I'm just like you."

"I think maybe you sell guns or something. And you don't respect the fact that Grim cares about me."

Lonnie laughed. "Grim wants to marry you. I'll bet you didn't even know that. We all want to marry you. You're great."

"Oh, please."

"O.K. I'll be quiet. Let's be quiet together. I'd like that."

She looked out the window, but Camaro wasn't at the cars. She couldn't remember whether or not she had locked the Buick. She considered the idea of Grim's wanting to marry her. She had tried to imagine it before, but it wasn't his style. At least she didn't think it was. It was certainly not hers. She thought she knew *that* for sure. She *had* locked the glove compartment.

She realized she was enjoying the scent of Lonnie's cologne, an expensive-seeming, green scent. He ate his bagel expertly, with big, neat bites and slow, clean chewing. The muscle in his jaw was like a pulse.

"What?"

"Nothing. Most of Grim's friends drive around in some kind of damaged luxury, like that Electra out there, like my used Corvette," she said, just to bug him. "So tell me, what do you do?"

"I adore bourgeois babies like you. I'm not a criminal, as the world leaders say. Not much, anyway." He put his napkin to his mouth, and draped it on his lap again. "Besides, Grim's a better player than I'll ever be. There's nothing damaged about any of his luxuries."

Butter stood up and unlooped her purse from the back of the chair. "I have to go."

Lonnie rose with her. "Me, too. Off to my mysterious trade."

She stopped to say good-bye to the owners of the restaurant, and then Lonnie held the door open as she went outside. "Thank you. Now, be a really good mystery and vanish."

"Oh, you're so pretty and mean. I love that. You remind me of my mother."

She still did not see Camaro. Noise from street traffic and a bread truck being unloaded at the grocery made it easier not to talk anymore to Lonnie. She thought Camaro must have sneaked off to the video store or the pet store, and she was grateful to have to look for her there rather than have to walk with Lonnie to their cars. The man stacking the bread crates onto a cart looked clean and strong, in tight blue shorts and a light blue shirt with the short sleeves rolled, like a delivery man on television. She stood watching him, waiting for Lonnie to walk off, but Lonnie put his hand on her back to urge her into the parking lot.

"Listen."

"What, Lonnie?"

"Do you hear that?"

Butter faltered. "What is it?"

"Give me your keys." Lonnie held out his hand.

"Hell no. Why?"

"Just give them to me, Butter." He grabbed the keys from her hand and trotted to the Buick.

"Come on, Lonnie. I don't have time for this tease."

He got behind the car, raised the trunk lid, and after a moment stepped to the side cradling Camaro.

"Damn it," Butter said. Lonnie set Camaro on her feet. Butter ran to her and felt her small damp face and arms until she was sure the girl was all right. She opened the passenger door and sat Camaro down on the seat. "You're supposed to be smart," Butter said.

Lonnie jogged back to the bagel shop and brought back a cup of water. Camaro drank half and said, "Oh, man, suppose you and this guy had gone to a motel or something. I might have died in there."

"*Why* were you in the trunk?" Butter asked.

"You can open some trunks from the inside, my daddy said. I thought this car was like that."

"You didn't have to scare me so thoroughly to find out."

"He must have meant from inside the passenger area —the trunk release," Lonnie said.

"No kidding," Camaro replied.

"We should call you Adventure Girl," said Lonnie, laughing. "A budding Houdini. Or, better yet, a fearless black-hole explorer. Yes, I see your future—Camaro, the intrepid galaxy voyager." He spread his arms out over his head, as if tracing the arc of the heavens.

"Hey, I get it," Camaro said, her eyes brightening. "Car stuff."

"Go home, Lonnie," Butter said. "Thanks and all that."

She strapped Camaro and herself in the Buick and headed back toward Sacred Lamb, leaving Lonnie in the parking lot. She tried to see the fun of what had just happened, as Lonnie had. Mrs. Mello—Rita—ought to have her fired or arrested. She wished she was on her way to see Grim, with whom all manner of catastrophe often seemed kept just distant enough to be a joke—except that this dangerous amusement was related to him. She considered throwing away the gun, but it wasn't hers, and maybe it was a fake gun. Anyway, it was locked up. Camaro suggested that they say nothing about either the trunk incident or the gun, and Butter explained why they had better tell the truth about everything. It was an opportune and easy lesson in honesty. But what she really wanted to say was that you can't trust anybody—not your teacher, your parents, even yourself.

They were on the interstate now. Camaro nudged Butter's knee and pointed out Butter's window. Butter turned to see a red-faced man with a yellow buzz cut driving an impeccable gray Cadillac right beside her at fifty-five miles per hour, his open white shirt collar flapping in the wind. He was motioning for her to roll down her window. Butter shook her head and gestured for him to pass, but he cranked his fist again. She sped up sluggishly and heard a rattling knock in the engine, the front end shook, and he stayed with her. Maybe he wanted to tell her about a fire in the tailpipe, she thought, or oil gushing from underneath. She slowed, rolled down her window, and he shouted something she couldn't catch. "What?" she yelled back, now wishing she could at least get to the gun.

"Just like it," he screamed, pointing, half-frowning and half-grinning, snarling maybe. "I'll sell you a car just like that one!"

"*This* one!"

"Exactly!"

"Cool," Camaro said. Butter laughed. She didn't know whether to try to pass him again or to slow down more and hope he passed her. The guy was crazy, obviously, offering her something she couldn't possibly want, that couldn't possibly be. She wanted something with rocket fuel, something ballistic. She was ready to blast away to escape this guy, leave this scene behind in trails of fiery smoke.

Power Burgers

GRIM COULD NOT explain his secrecy to Butter. Concealing Rita was a prank, a surprise, he said. He wanted them to meet and to be enchanted. He wanted to orchestrate chance. Butter wouldn't accept that; she didn't like feeling used. And what about the gun? Although the gun was not his fault, he took the blame and passed it on in private to Belly Man, who promised better care. Grim was in trouble for a while, and so was Camaro for getting inside the trunk. Butter was contrite before Rita but nobody blamed her. She said little about Lonnie. Camaro raved about his car but the grown-ups seemed disinterested. The incident helped them to know one another and Rita settled in. They bought the Hell's Angels' house— Mr. Brown's old place—still the biggest one around.

Two years later Camaro had shown she was smart. She had made her A's and that summer she got a job at Grim's place. One day from his screened front porch she glanced through the doorway to check the police scanner sitting on an end table in the living room. She then got up from the cracked vinyl sofa and went outside to tend the hamburgers shrinking on the grill by the front stoop. She was gentle with the porch's torn screen door so as not to disturb Grim's talk with Belly Man. Belly Man wanted to renegotiate the contract to clean the two tow trucks Grim owned and the used cars that Grim sometimes had for sale. They stood by the trucks in the driveway bordering a wide weedy yard reserved for parking. Grim leaned against the front headlight of the big Jerr-Dan, with his hands in his pockets and his head down, looking doubtful, while Belly Man walked around the truck, apparently figuring how much soap and water would be required. The sticking points were that Belly Man wanted the tow trucks and cars delivered to him and that he wanted a flat monthly fee no matter how many cars he washed; Grim argued that he sometimes had no cars at all to sell.

Camaro was about to turn twelve. It had recently hit her with startling clarity that Grim was her mother's actual blood relative. She had known it, of course, but was fully awake to it now. So she had pestered her parents to let her work down at Grim's to earn a little money, though her intent was really to study him. She thought scrutiny of him would help her understand her mother. How could they be related, her mother and him?

One morning near the end of the school year she had sat alone in her living room and watched her father and Grim on the porch discussing something, and Grim laughed out loud so open and strong that the sound reached her through the closed window. Her mother was frequently amused but she seldom laughed so loud, never with the raucous surprise of her uncle Grim. Her mother seemed always to know ahead of time what was funny. Camaro had lately collected two new words for her, "dour" and "urbane"—her mother was too sophisticated to make Uncle Grim's kind of noise. She had taken the words from a pre-SAT study booklet in her school's library, and they each had a place waiting in her consciousness. They seemed to fit her mother like eggs in a carton, and helped her to balance her mother in her head. She had other words, too, like "elegant," "pulchritudinous," "obdurate" and "serene." None of these words fit Uncle Grim. And Camaro wondered with self-conscious maturity how two people from the same parents and same place could turn out so different. It made her own future—as an adopted child with no idea about her biological relatives—almost unbearably open, the choices overwhelmingly unlimited. As awesomely mysterious as her birth.

Belly Man was repeating that bringing the cars to his facility would save Grim money on the cleaning charge. Grim was looking at his boots and chuckling.

"I gotta get somebody to drive them, Belly. I gotta pay that somebody. I don't mind doing that, but then I gotta pay you all that money whether anything's dirty or not."

"Grim, you must think this is Wild West days when everything costed a nickel."

"I know what today is. All I'm saying is that we ought to be trying to help each other here instead of putting each other out of business."

"Well, what do you think I'm doing? I need the business, you need clean vehicles so let's hook this up. What's the big stinking problem?"

Grim raised his gaze to Belly Man standing next to the R in "Power." It was painted in red-orange script on the side of the truck and ringed by a jagged burst of glittering yellow. "I guess you're right. I ought to be more optimistic. I can't be doing business and expecting the worst, can I? Even if you're the one I'm doing business with." Grim took his right hand from his pocket and held it out. Belly Man shook it and grinned.

"This is a good deal, Grim Power."

"I guarantee it." Grim straightened up.

"All right, all right. Now let me tell you something. I keeps smelling hamburgers."

Camaro took the four cooked burgers off the grill and placed them on the upper rack. Then she put the remaining four pink patties over the coals. A red Firebird and a black Quad-4 raced loudly up the two-lane road in front of the house. Grim and Belly Man spread out the car washing contract on the hood of a truck and started crossing out and adding stuff they had agreed.

Belly Man wore a burgundy rayon short set and sandals with burgundy ribbed socks, Grim wore denim clothes and brown boots. That crack from Belly Man about Wild

West days had to do with Grim's former life as a local cowboy star. He rode a yellow palomino in parades and at church bazaars, and wore a tight black cowboy suit with long white fringe. He was in his late twenties then. Camaro's mom had disapproved. He'd embarrassed her, she told Camaro, a grown man who, in the age of space travel, pranced on a horse up the street in his Western getup. Once, after her parents had gotten married and moved from town, they saw him on a nationally televised amateur show doing lasso stunts. Years later, when Grim started the towing business, Rita had to get used to another embarrassment—the idea of a tow truck tooling along the streets with her own last name blazing from the side. But at least she hadn't had to see it, living then in Massachusetts. She had expected much more of her brother.

Camaro vaguely understood that she was being warned of what was expected of her. Still, she saw no current evidence of her mother's embarrassment by her brother, or her disapproval of his business. Her mother now seemed rather proud of him, and had only expressed worry about the kind of people who might come around. But her daddy said it would be all right, that Camaro needed a job, that he wished Grim would hire her three younger sisters, too. Her mother had smiled in her knowing way and Camaro went to work.

Camaro peppered the hamburgers meant for an early dinner with Grim and Butter, who still taught first grade and lived in a condo about two miles from Grim. She had promised to come over with color samples and fabric swatches for the new playroom and bedroom Grim had added to the back of the old house. Camaro thought the annex, a cedar-sided A-frame, made the main, green-painted shingle-sided house shabbier; it was actually three rooms, including an enclosed pool, which Camaro and her sisters were fond of. Grim planned to have dinner and then watch a movie with Butter, while Camaro monitored towing calls. But if this Saturday was like last Saturday, a mixed group of Grim's friends and associates would show up after dusk to hang around the pool. Grim would likely ride out on one or two crash or breakdown calls while his friends swam or played cards. And Camaro would fetch chips and ice under Butter's watch, and also her father's, who would wander in for a card game, just to see how things were going. Right now, from her place at the grill, she could see the police scanner flashing, putting out static and low-volume garble.

"You know Belly Man," Grim said to Camaro. They had stepped over to the stoop, Belly Man folding the contract into a rectangle and slipping it into his shirt pocket. Camaro shifted the spatula to her left hand in case Belly Man wanted to shake. He didn't.

"Everything OK?" Camaro asked.

"Dandy," Grim said. His smile spread into his long sideburns—holdovers from the buckaroo days. "This is a crafty dude."

"You got me wrong," Belly Man said. "I ain't crafty."

"What are you talking about? I got you perfectly. You got *me* wrong."

"How do I got you?"

"Wrong," said Grim.

A sly smiled crossed Belly Man's fleshy face. "What's 'wrong' mean, anyway?"

Grim laughed. "See? That's right. There's no meaning

even to speak of. That's my point. There's only value, like me and you just made. You're crafty, I'm crafty, we're all crafty, and all like that. At least we'd better be. That's all I'm saying."

"Man, I don't now what the *hell* you're saying."

"Yeah, you're a trip. You're the bo-bo. I can't handle it." Grim shoved his hands into his back pockets and brushed his boot toe on his pants leg.

"Hey."

Grim chuckled. "Say hello to Camaro. You all excuse me." He squeezed Camaro's shoulder. "Tell him what I'm talking about, Camaro." He nodded to Belly Man, went up the steps to the screen door and disappeared. Camaro recognized this maneuver. When Grim had no more time for, or was bored with, someone, he introduced him to Camaro.

Camaro already knew about Belly Man as somebody her mother used to teach, a long time ago before she and her daddy got married. They had run into him at the grocery store when they moved here two years ago. And they would see him now and again around town. One time when her mother was in the hospital back in the old days, Belly Man had visited her. Her mother had never forgotten. But Camaro was a little scared of him. At the grocery store he'd paid little attention to her and her sisters, and winked at her mother as he went away down the paper-towel aisle. And then last Saturday he was among the crowd lounging around Grim's pool, talking to her daddy.

Today he tilted his burgundy Kangol cap and stared at the meat on the grill.

"Want one?"

"They looks rather small, don't they?"

"Want two?"

"Yeah," putting his hands on his oversized stomach. He wore a garnet ring and a nugget watch with a red face. "That'd be about right for the Belly Man. They done yet?"

"You're in a hurry, I guess."

"I run a business, li'l girl. You know that."

Camaro took a couple of buns out of the bag on the side shelf of the grill and squeezed mustard on them. "You used to travel some, didn't you, Mr. Belly Man? I heard Uncle Grim say you went away for a while."

"Whatchu talking about? I was up at state for a year or so awhile back some. Then I was on parole and probation for another year. Otherwise I ain't been nowhere. You don't know about that manslaughter charge?"

"Oh, yeah." She vaguely remembered now, her mother and father talking about it maybe. But she couldn't distinguish it from any number of local misfortunes she had heard about. She spied the tuft of hair just under Belly Man's bottom lip, and shuddered. Who had Belly Man killed, she wondered.

"Well, it was an accident, you know. Anyway, the judge said for me not to associate with any known criminals. I said to the judge, 'Criminals you know or ciminals I know?' I said, 'Judge, that means I can't see none of my friends. I can't even go home!' That didn't make no difference to the judge. I was real low profile, that's all. But I'm way back now, big time."

Camaro heard Grim, who must have been eavesdropping, laughing in the kitchen. Then she heard the portable phone ring on the porch. Handing the buns to Belly Man, she rushed to answer it. She took the phone into the kitchen, where Grim passed her on his way to the back bathroom; and through the window she could see Belly Man scooping up a hamburger and making a sandwich. "Power Wrecker," she said into the receiver.

"Power Towing!" Grim hollered from the back. "Read the damn truck door, Camaro. Read the Yellow Pages!"

It was Butter on the phone. "Let me tell you something about Power, Camaro," she said in a fake deep voice. "Power's something you take!"

"You must have seen a 'Dallas' rerun last night," Camaro said.

"Nope. It's a commercial. Can't get it out of my head. Commercials use your mind without your permission; remember that."

"You want to talk to Uncle Grim?"

"No. I want to know what he smells like."

"I'll get him." She put the receiver to her thigh and yelled to Grim, and he yelled back that he was shaving.

"He's standing right here," Camaro said into the phone, "and he has a sort of manly smell. Spicy, woodsy, leathery. And he's eating an orange."

"Oooo," Butter said. "I'm like butter now."

"Very punny."

"Don't call me punny. Tell him I'm delayed here at home. I'm cutting my hair. Bye."

Grim yelled back, "What does she want?"

"She'll be late," Camaro said, hanging up.

Through the window she watched Belly Man make a second sandwich and decided to wait inside until he finished eating it. Maybe he would get the message that no one was coming back to say good-bye, and leave. Her daddy had said he used to be a bully. Well, yeah, she thought. He had killed somebody, and seemed not to even mind it. How could he not be surprised that his life had turned out like that? She thought a person had to be just plain bad to accept bad luck with such disinterest. She couldn't imagine why he'd visited her mother in the hospital, and didn't really believe it, anymore than she could imagine the Hell's Angels living in her house, or believe in the story about her mother's running the Hell's Angels out. Belly Man, she thought, couldn't really care about anybody.

When Belly Man began making a third sandwich, Camaro went back outside. "That'll be five dollars."

"Yeah, right," Belly Man said through the food in his mouth.

"Grim's expecting company, that's all. This isn't a public picnic."

"Look, Camaro, I ain't no public. Me and Grim just signed a contract. You ain't got to act like the police just 'cause you got a job. What you got to drink?"

"You're about to eat everything I cooked."

"Well cook some more. I'll still be hungry and Grim don't mind. He couldn't do nothing if he did, no way. Just like you."

Grim came banging out the porch door with his car keys in his hand. "I have to go to the mall right quick. You look thirsty, Belly. Camaro, get him something to drink. Butter will be here in a minute. Tell her I'll be back." He got in his '63 Ford and pulled away. Camaro watched the car, immaculate and black, which she had helped polish that very morning, disappear beyond the neighbor's houses up the road.

"See, he don't mind. Or he's a sucker. Or both."

"Don't talk that way about Uncle Grim."

"I got *some* rights."

"He likes you, for some reason."

"So? I like him, too."

"So you think you're taking advantage of him."

"So, I can't think?"

A horn tooted on the road and Camaro looked up in time to see a primer-covered pickup tear by. The driver waved but Camaro didn't see who it was. She went into the house to avoid looking at Belly Man.

"A beer'd be about right. I'm gone celebrate," Belly Man shouted.

Camaro considered shouting back—something about Belly's Man's being in a hurry; something about his mother, whoever she was, but she stopped herself. That was not how Grim would handle it, or her mother. She paused in front of the open refrigerator and breathed in the cold air. At least a case worth of different brands of beer crowded the shelves, along with cans of biscuits, cantaloupe halves, a two-dozen egg carton, tossed salad in a large glass bowl, a two-liter bottle of red drink, and a plastic-wrapped plate of sliced tomato and onion. She wished Grim hadn't left. How could he leave a minor alone with Belly Man? Whatever Grim had to do at the mall, he'd probably spend some extra time at a newsstand reading classic-car magazines. She wished Butter would hurry up. She slammed the refrigerator door and stalked back to the new rooms. She didn't understand people like Belly Man. Let the greasy killer eat all the food. Let him choke.

She passed the unfinished bedroom on one side of a hall and the unfinished playroom on the other side and headed straight through the gymnasium-style doors for the pool. She considered going right out the sliding glass door and escaping through the wooded lot to her house. Her mother and sisters would be home, the cleaning and shopping finished now that the gold of twilight had begun. If she went home, she'd talk about Belly Man and her mother would get mad at Grim for leaving her with him, and get mad at her for letting Grim leave, and forbid her going back down there again. Camaro got mad at herself. She should be able to deal with people like Belly Man. Apparently everybody else in her family could.

Light poured through the windows that traced the top of the white plaster walls. Camaro ran her hand through the blue water of the pool. It was warm. The spa was steaming, no need to test that. What would you call Belly Man? A manslaughterer? That would be interesting on a résumé. Or a smug assassin who somehow owned a car wash despite a prison record and probation, or parole, or whatever? Camaro flopped onto an aqua-cushioned lounge chair. It let out a receding hiss that eventually lost itself in the gurgle of the pool drain.

She felt mocked by these acquiescent sounds, and the whole watery room. It wasn't just Belly Man making her angry; it was her uncle Grim. She suddenly saw him as her mother had. Grim being the fool doffing his hat from his horse, Grim in that tow truck and loading his yard with junk cars, Grim making her name—her mother's name—the emblem of the ridiculous, the symbol of lameness and loss.

Camaro hated that nothing seemed stable. That even if you weren't adopted, nothing was really sure. Her mother's mother was dead, having driven herself off a bridge, they said. Her mother's father was never spoken of—alive somewhere, they thought. Her mother's strength sometimes seemed more like snobbery, and although her father seemed solid, she wondered how *long* he would seem so to her. Already it seemed stupid for him to let her work at Uncle Grim's. And was Uncle Grim's generosity a real triumph, a real transcendence over the uncertainty of things, or the dumb bliss of a patsy? After all, Belly Man's meanness seemed to keep *him* feeling just as content.

Camaro got up off the lounge chair and headed back toward the old part of the house. Maybe Belly Man had finally left. When she got back to the kitchen and looked out the window, he was sitting by the grill on a lawn chair from the porch. He held a bottle of beer, and Butter was handing him a hamburger. Her hair was much shorter and she wore big silver circle earrings. She turned toward Camaro, looking fresh and stunning, and said, "I see you in that window, Camaro. Who's in charge here?"

"I am." She came out into the yard and noticed that all the food was gone except the burger that Belly Man was biting into. "I must be a pretty good cook"—trying not to sound confounded for Butter.

Belly Man grunted while he eyed Camaro and chewed. "I believe the li'l girl got mad at me."

"Naughty Camaro," Butter said, teasing.

"My job ought to be sweeping, exclusively. I could be the best sweeper in town. I'm no good at figuring out how Mr. Belly Man rates eating up all our stuff."

"Business should be a pleasure, Camaro. Isn't that Grim's motto? And the Belly Man here is a valued member of the community."

"Who in the community did you kill, anyway?"

"Camaro," Butter said, reproaching. "Don't be rude."

Belly Man held his hands up with his elbows resting on the armrests of the lawn chair, the half-eaten hamburger in one hand and the nearly full beer in the other. His scarred, heavy legs were crossed. "Life's too short, sweetmeat. Everybody's got some kind of allergy, can't breathe right, maybe. So many, many peoples with limps, bad ankles and wrenched knees. Sometimes they hits their heads. It don't take much to die, whether you trying for it or not. Some folks you can just scare to death."

"What the hell do you mean by that?" Butter asked. She held his gaze a few seconds, frowning. "You're supposed to be a jolly old fat man."

"Oh, I'm just philosophizing. I picked up pondering fate when I was at the big house."

"Well, you can go on home and do that. Camaro and I have some things to do. And Grim, too. We'll have to see you later."

"I do have a business." He raised himself up. "Gotta go." He touched the short bill of his cap with the mouth of the beer bottle and nodded. "Sweet Butter. Sweetmeat," he said to Camaro.

They watched him drive away, still with the burger and beer, and then Butter sank into the lawn chair. Her toenails were pearly pink. "Belly Man will exhaust you. You shouldn't worry about him eating all the dinner, and don't worry about Grim blaming you for it. He knows what's what."

Camaro stared at the empty grill and the empty bun bag laying flat under the squeeze mustard. "Well what *is* what?"

Butter laughed lightly. "Good question."

"I mean, damn, Uncle Grim's the one who doesn't know what's going on. Everybody can see that."

"Why are you mad at Grim? Belly Man is the bad guy today. You can see he's probably always unruly around food. Actually, the man he killed, accidentally of course, had just eaten up some of Belly Man's French fries at a ball game, without permission. That's what Grim said."

Camaro considered that awhile. She started to snicker. "Best to let him eat, I suppose." She decided to let the subject of Grim stay dropped. She couldn't explain it to Butter anyway.

"Right. Don't be so bothered." Butter smiled up at her, as if that was enough to buttress her until she figured out how to live. It was a lovely smile, and she envisioned for a moment that if Butter were her real mother, it would be something unwavering she could build on.

She listened to an engine wind and downshift in the distance. She watched the road in front of Grim's house for speeding things rushing by. The clouds in the sunset were bright orange, more orange than Camaro had ever seen, and a deep orange dusk glowed in the pines and leafy oaks across the street.

"Look at that," she said to Butter just as a gold-painted,

Gold Wing motorcycle with more lights and reflectors than the tow trucks coasted into the driveway. It was Grim, in a metallic gold helmet. He slipped the big bike all the way up to the grill and shut the motor. "It's a tryout," he said, grinning. "They got a show going on at the mall."

"I like the color, at least," Butter said. "But don't say you're keeping that thing."

Grim pulled off the helmet and frowned at her. "You cut your hair down to nothing," he said.

She turned to Camaro and asked, "How do you like it?"

Camaro didn't know if she meant the haircut or the bike.

"Yeah," said Grim, "what do you think?"

Rita's Luminous Mystery

A YEAR PASSED. Mayes rose to speak at the A.A. meeting, his first time. My name is Mayes Mello and I'm an alcoholic. People applauded. Mayes, thought, Well *maybe* I'm an alcoholic, but it was too late to take it back. He didn't want to disappoint. He had become very impressed with the people attending the meetings. They were all wondrous. He had something he wanted to tell them, about the power they knew and relied on, and how it was manifested to him.

My wife is Jesus, he said. He chuckled. Just kidding.

What I mean is that Rita is *like* Jesus. She has a quality. She's extraordinary. Yet, my Rita says that, no matter what, you cannot plan your life. Did Jesus ever say a thing like that? I don't think so. Jesus understood something other. I don't know that Rita means it; she might be only trying to fit in with all of us unenlightened ones. I mean, even I know that to at least some extent you can plan your life. For instance, if you eat a cake a week you get fat, so you can plan to get fat that way or you can plan not to. I plan not to, for instance. Or, if I want to know how a metal alloy behaves at sixty below, I drop the temp on that sucker and watch it crack. I'm a cryophysicist, and I'm sitting O.K., having gone from high school science-teaching, through the higher academia—specimen that I was—to practical research on the behavior of mass in the too-cold climates of space. I planned the whole trip. Rita, I should think, ought to respect that.

Jesus said that what you do now determines how you will be later. That's what he meant; to know the future, study today, what goes around comes around, you reap what you sow. I believe that. Anybody just glancing ought to see that it's pure common sense. But Rita, my wife, is like Jesus in that she does everything right instinctively. She is like the Buddhas and bodhisattvas I've read about. She's got a really good heart is what I mean, and she loves everybody. Even the guy that kidnapped her. That's what I'm trying to get the police to understand. Rita is originally sinless.

She asks, What past event, what past present, led to her being abducted, assaulted, and then arrested for public drunkenness—for drunk driving—and caused her picture to be in the paper, her arrest on television? She was on her way to work, damn it.

She doesn't think anyone believes her. She doesn't blame anyone, really; she understands how it looks. She was drunk, and driving. But she expects people to be charitable, to believe the truth. I can tell she even suspects me of doubting her because sometimes she cries and she won't let me comfort her. She quotes to me my belief in cause and effect—if she's in trouble, then she caused it—assumes my complete faith in that logic. I admit, I don't understand.

The police, of course, and the D.A. certainly think she's lying. Her lawyer, maybe he believes and maybe he doesn't. He keeps asking her to tell the story again. Did anybody see her in the car with the guy? Did she phone anyone at work before leaving home that morning? Is there anyone—a neighbor, me, the paper boy—who can say that she even intended to go to work, that she's telling the truth? I tell them, yes, she's telling the truth, she intended to go to work.

Still, she's a drinker. All our friends know that. But she's not a drunk. She doesn't get drunk in the morning and miss work. She couldn't keep a job that way, not a teaching job anyway. She's called in a few times and gotten substitutes, but for the flu, like anybody else. Now her principal is hinting that her calls have had a pattern. Monday-morning calls. He's said that maybe now that she's gotten this attention she can get the help she needs. The head of our library branch, where Rita tells stories to the preschoolers on Saturday mornings, has suggested that she discontinue her visits until this is all straightened out.

So she's putting up with this suspicion and betrayal, and she loves and forgives the principal, the librarian, and especially the guy that's done this to her. If we can just find him, everything would be better.

But Rita only half wants to find him. Certainly she doesn't like being thought a liar, and it's embarrassing— indeed stunning—being perceived as someone you absolutely are not. But she knows the man is in pain and would not want to cause him any more. The police aren't even looking for him. When they question her, I question them. She tells the same story every time, a little different here and there as she remembers things, forgets things, finds something or other more or less important.

She was just two blocks from home, at the traffic light, and she saw the man coming in the side mirror. But she didn't think to do anything. Her door was unlocked. Bums are always on the corners, and the only thing different was that he was in her mirror this time, coming up beside the car. That was strange, and when she thought to run the light or lock the door it was too late. He was pushing her over onto the passenger seat. His odor paralyzed her, shocked her, made her cringe. He smelled like excrement. Like excrement and B.O. and rotten teeth. And *he* must have run the light, because she realized they were speeding, the world outside the car blurring by.

He wore an unbuttoned blue shirt with green stripes tucked into beltless pants, and the dark skin of his chest was ashy gray. It was cold that morning, frost on the windows not yet fully melted by the heater. She had on her coat and gloves and a knit hat and scarf. His pants were filthy, the color of tobacco with black stains like grease and white stains like snot. His shoes were badly scuffed wing tips with no laces, and he didn't have socks on his gray, cracked ankles. He reached inside his shirt and pulled out a gun. It had a short barrel. That's when he looked at her, sidelong with huge watery eyes.

"I'll kill you."

"No."

He cursed her viciously, vulgarly.

His stink so strong it was in her ears. She vomited.

"Looks like you had breakfast." He snorted a laugh. "You got to clean that mess up. I ain't gone be riding round in no puke car."

"Let me out," she breathed.

"I'll kill you. Messing up my day with this mess." He shook the gun at her and put it back in his shirt. As always, she had flung her purse and briefcase on the backseat. She wanted to reach to the backseat for a tissue from her purse, but she didn't want to call attention to herself. She thought about his stealing her money and credit cards, and the hassle of canceling everything.

But she was embarrassed by the vomiting, so she reached for the purse. He grabbed her arm and snatched the bag. The car swerved, nearly hit a truck in the next lane, and he caught the wheel and straightened. She tried on the spot to remember that truck, but couldn't. Immediately it had no color. It was gone. The man took from the purse her fat wallet filled with receipts, cards, photos. He turned the bag over and flung it around. Pens, makeup, gum, checkbook and tissue scattered over the seat and her lap, landed in the pool at her feet.

She wiped her mouth with a tissue, dried between her

fingers, cleaned the dashboard as best she could. She thought about me, she says, and our daughters. She felt sorry for us, who wouldn't know what had happened to her, where she was—who'd learn maybe months later that the skeleton found in the distant woods belonged to his missing wife, their missing mother. Black female, mid-to-late fifties. And imagining that made it all seem unreal to her, as if she were predicting the end of a made-up mystery.

When Rita tells her library stories, you feel as though you are in them. This is because when she tells them *she* is in them. You sense that in front of her eyes there is a transparent screen on which her tales live, and through which she observes her audience. And the audience, through the service of the same transparent screen, observes the tale and the teller. She stands there wearing her caftan, waving her cow-tail switch, and the myth of the origin of sleep awakens, or the story of the clever spider and the palm gourd begins to creep and speak of itself.

Yet she is holding something back from the police and her attorney, and that is why they don't believe her. I do my best to persuade them to speak without saying what she doesn't want me to say. We differ about what should be known, although even if I could tell anything, my power to persuade would be less than hers.

It has been a month since the mystery. She yelps in her sleep. Usually I wake her as soon as she starts, but once I was in the basement washing a late-night load of clothes when I heard her. She got so loud I was honestly surprised she couldn't wake herself. I shake her, is what I do. She stops with a grunt, and a whimper. Always, somebody is chasing her. That son of a bitch. Yet, she seems afraid only when sleeping. When awake, she's angry, disappointed, but laughing and forgiving.

I used to say, Rita never meets a stranger. She's become good friends over the phone with the wife of the man who delivered our living-room tables last year, when we redecorated. I don't know how it happened. She'd never seen this woman in person, just some photographs the delivery man showed her. She served the guy ham sandwiches and tea for lunch and looked at his snapshots, and somehow she's talking to his wife about who knows what. Troubles, it turns out. Their teenager daughter was pregnant. Later we sent the baby some toys. We gave them some money when the guy had a heart attack.

She has invited people over at the least provocation. She meets someone from Ontario, for example, where we used to live, gives them our address and tells them to come by anytime, as if we all have so much in common. If she meets someone who is going to Ontario, she gives them our old neighbors' addresses. So far none of these strangers has actually shown up at our door, and I don't know who has visited our old neighbors at my wife's insistence. I tell her it's dangerous to be so open, so giving, so trusting. She thinks I'm saying you're not supposed to like people so much. Maybe I am. She could be inviting over a killer, a robber, a vampire. I should hope that during her kidnaping she did not invite the kidnapper to our home, this man she dreams about.

She told me that after she got sick, when they were out of the traffic on the outskirts of town, she felt hot, and realized that the heater was on full blast. She switched it

off and yanked loose her scarf, pulled off her gloves, unbuttoned her coat. She tried to breathe deep but the smells
stopped her. She wanted to lower a window, but looked
at the man and realized he would be cold. His knuckles
were scabbed, his fingers long and creased. The stubble
on his face seemed as stiff and black as brush bristles, some
of them ingrown; puss-filled bumps dotted his cheek and
chin. He was skinny but muscled, like a scavenger animal,
a hyena. Hair grew thick down his neck.

He steered the car onto a ramp to the interstate, heading
west. As the ramp rose and they sped along the bridge
across the river, she gazed out over the top of the town
—churches, schools, houses, office buildings. She thought,
This is what it's like to die, leaving everything familiar,
accelerating, unable to stop.

He drove way out of town, got on some narrow back
roads that split fields of dried cornstalks. She tried to talk
to him and he cursed her. Cursed her for hours. Around
ten he made her buy bourbon at a rural package store and
forced her to drink it with him as they drove empty two-
lanes. They drank in a parking lot of an abandoned gas
station along some piney country road. The concrete lot
was crumbling, tough old winter weeds grizzled in the
cracks. She tried not to swallow the liquor, but he held
the gun to her throat and ordered her. She swallowed
what she dared and then he drank some. They took turns
like that. It was a half-gallon bottle. He raised the tilt
wheel out of the way, leaned their seats back some.

As I said, Rita knows how to drink. First of all, she
made it look like she was swallowing a lot but she wasn't,
and second, alcohol doesn't go straight to her head. She

can hold it pretty well. She had a lot by now, though, and it was creeping up on her. She could sense the man was feeling better. It was clear that he relied on alcohol to ease his pain. She was worried he'd get the idea to rape her.

She began to imagine that when he drank he left some of his pain in the bottle; and when she drank she first swallowed his pain away and then breathed in her well-being. That was the exchange—his pain for her health. And he became jollier. He said they were going to drive to Las Vegas, spend her money, and when the money ran out they would use her shining credit. He said she could buy him a house on a lake, in Africa, on Lake Victoria, and what kind of name for an African lake was that?

"What's your name?" she asked.

He let out a breath, let his chin slump to his chest, the bottle between his legs. He told her to get out of the car, and as she did he got out too, came around to her. The wind was whipping—ballooning and flapping his open shirt and molding his pants to his pipe-thin legs.

Straight on, he had a wide face, winglike cheekbones, eyebrows that met in a V in the middle, and beautifully shaped, cold-white lips. He hit her. She ducked and his fist grazed and split her eyebrow. She fell back against the car and he rushed her, groping for her breasts through her coat. She felt nothing much, random and unpleasant pressure, as if drugged and submitting to a foul-smelling search. Then, as if bored, as if he could not be satisfied, could not make himself felt, he gave up, let his arms go limp as he leaned on her and breathed into her knit hat.

He rolled off and pushed back, arms pinwheeling like a stumbling cow-town drunk. He ran trip-toed away from her but stopped, wavering, at the corner of the building. He turned and, in afterthought, pulled his gun and pointed at her with the length of his arms. For seconds he steadied it, and then he backed away and disappeared.

But while he had stood there sighting her, she had seen a radiance about him, a gleaming silver-gold sheen issuing from him like the spiny fins of a phosphorescent fish.

After he was gone the whole scene was radiant—the tall, dry pale grass in the ditch across the road, the black bending pine trees with their silver-needle quills, the disintegrating parking lot, the glowing rust of the gas pumps, the white concrete-block building. She took her glasses from her coat pocket and put them on to verify what she was seeing. The car was the most beautiful she had seen it, the paint like a clear green glaze over chrome.

Light was in everything during her drive away from there, during her woozy, disoriented search for a phone booth. She doesn't know how long she drove before she slammed into a tinseled, shimmering tree that seemed to swoon out of the middle of the road. The road had seemed as bright and straight as a sheet of glass.

The police believe her bleeding head resulted from the wreck. She wasn't wearing a seat belt. There is little evidence of the man. There were fingerprints other than hers found on the half-empty bottle, but Rita can't remember where they bought it, and the police say the prints could belong to the salesman. They don't match any known criminal's. No distinct suspicious prints anywhere else, not even on the purse, not that the police looked very hard. Nor can she remember where the old gas station is, despite our drives around to look for it.

So, right now, it doesn't look good for Rita legally. She failed big-time on the Breathalyzer. She won't tell the police about the vision, refusing to be ridiculed for something as powerful as that, and sad that it would have to be received with the knowledge that she was drunk. She was plastered, blitzed, looped. If she had planned it, she says, there would be no suspicion attached. If she had planned it, she would be in control. Nothing, she says, can account for what she's gone through.

But I tell them, for her faith in me and for my faith in her, that she was not injured in the car wreck. That bruise is no steering wheel mark over her eye. In fact, she remembers something the police could verify. When the state trooper found her, she was sitting upright behind the wheel, the front end accordioned, the motor running and the heater on low. Her eyeglasses were on the floor between her feet, neatly folded, reflecting blue-white light back at her, as if placed there for her, for when she was ready for the whole truth to be revealed, again.

Something Scrambled

LONNIE WELCOME DESIGNED boxes for a product design firm. Yes, he was an attorney and small entrepreneur,
but his grandfather once owned part of the firm, which
worked closely with the ad agency still partly owned by
the family. So Lonnie got to do art. Mostly he did the
cover art, though occasionally he worked with shapes if
the product called for something nonstandard. He headed
a team.

Once, in May—the spring after Rita's disagreement
with the law—he was taking a week off, ostensibly to

work undistracted on a new pencil-sharpener box. But he lay on his chocolate leather sofa considering the transformation of Butter. It was the first day of his working vacation. Monday. But almost everyone was off because it was Memorial Day. Butter and he were supposed to have lunch. In the four years he'd known her, since she had moved to town, she had changed from the stylishly, prim primary school teacher to a succulently plump seductress. And it seemed to have happened overnight, as astonishing and complete as Gregor Samsa's up and at 'em as a bug.

He had heard of Nazis and Klansmen who suddenly stopped being bigots to marry black people or Jews. He had known drug addicts who got clean, two who simply found Jesus and started shaving extra close—starched collars and dark suits on Wednesdays and Sundays, a few who with some unnamed power could look a loaded crack pipe in the eye and say no. Lonnie, too, had turned around. Not very long before, four and a half years, he would wake up cotton-brained, put on tennis shorts to go to a deli and drink beer all morning, then ride his bike down to his father's apartments to collect rent and heroin from the tenants. He already had the law degree but had lost his job at the D.A.'s office. He was stealing from his father—forging some of his checks and prescriptions, lifting from the pharmacy closet at his dental office—and shooting smack in the upstairs bathroom at home. Smoking coke sometimes late at night. Now—who would have thought—he had the design degree and the good job, plus the small, immaculate house bought from the architect who renovated it. He rarely drank now, Russian vodka and good tequila. They were closest to the clean, white pharmaceutical tastes he used to crave. It was his only indulgence.

He had decided not to die without having done something honest and good. His first goal had been to simply stop doing bad. Butter's was more mysterious, like that of the suddenly enlightened Nazi, and physical. The biggest surprise: She had started being naughty with Lonnie, which would have been savory if he had not suspended his serious flirtation with her. Part of the self-imposed discipline to build the strongest willpower. She had been on his list of pleasures to quit until he was sure he had really quit drugs. Replacing the vanity of consumption with the vanity of refusal seemed to make him attractive.

Butter had taken a summer receptionist job in the office of the attorney Lonnie had hired to set up a trust fund for his fifteen-year-old sister. Catholic school teaching didn't pay Butter very well. When Lonnie stepped off the elevator for his appointment, she was behind the front desk, smiling, expecting him. He was surprised, and very taken with her clear brown eyes. His own muddied eyes were only gradually clearing of the trauma of drug-induced visions, and the relative innocence of hers was heartening. They reminded him of his sister's, which he had not seen in several months. Butter wore a cream linen shirt. Her young dark skin, her dimpled cheek, seemed very soft, as though easily bruised, and as smooth and supple as warm dough. She extended an almost unbearable arm to shake his hand, firmly.

"Hi, Lonnie. You're on perfect time."

"Good. Why are you here?"

She told him with none of the tough-girl coldness she usually gave him.

On her desk was a heart-shaped frame of her and Grim embracing against a mountainscape. An old picture, a winter scene, her bare head close-cropped and Grim in the buckskin cowboy hat he used to wear. Lonnie remembered that mountain vacation. He was making his rounds one night and had stumbled upon Grim's house when the slides were being shown. In the picture, Grim had on heavy-rimmed, yellow-lens Blu Blockers. He looked much too happy with her. She looked much too young for him.

She now picked up the telephone and rang Lonnie's attorney, who came out personally. He was a friend of Lonnie's ruined uncle, himself a lawyer, retired. This man was scary—suave and thin with straight oiled hair and fine red skin. He wore a great soft suit and his eyes were green. He said in a quite sincere-sounding voice, "Taking care, Lonnie? Taking quite good care? May God bless you." Nevertheless, Lonnie liked him, and maybe through him or from paperwork on his desk Butter had learned about Lonnie's effort, and maybe that is why she was finally friendly.

He lay on the sofa thinking about that, and watching the early light swell the sheer white curtains in the window. He turned on the *Today* show. Bryant and Katie were wearing matching tan clothes. Outside, the local handyman, Jonah, cranked up the gas-powered tiller Lonnie had rented to turn over the yard. He'd driven over from his boardinghouse on the avenue nearby. Last week he'd finished the front yard, and already something green was poking through the straw he'd laid down. It didn't look like grass, though, but Lonnie was being optimistic. The phone rang and he fumbled with the rubber buttons on the TV remote pad, trying to lower the volume before he picked up the receiver, which was not beside him on the sofa cusion or on the table beside the sofa, but on its cradle in the kitchen. By the time he picked up, before the voice mail caught it, he had a dial tone.

He took the phone back to the living room and made a discovery. He had not lowered the volume but had changed the channel to something scrambled. A bare breast twisted and flickered on the screen, then distorted flashes of what looked like other body parts. A faint, woman's voice praised a thing call "the tongue," on sale for $59.00, reduced from $79.00. He had a home-shopping sex show. The woman said the tongue was worth $509.00 for all the pleasure it provided. Just add a little oil, she said, since it was without its own saliva, and minus lips. The spokeswoman's image writhed and surfaced in the wriggling bands on the screen. She was a tough-looking curly brunette, as frenetically broken up as a Picasso woman—if Picasso had used electronics—in a laced, black-leather, heart-shaped bodice.

The phone rang again. Lonnie thought it might be his team assistant, who was erratic lately, very weepy and wanting advice, since her husband, who worked in marketing, had begun courting one of the interns. One reason Lonnie was taking the week off was to avoid such intrigues, including the sticky rumor that the president of the firm, whose wedding he had attended his second week on the job, already had a wife, had in fact two households, two lives in the same town. Taking the job was now seeming like a bad idea. He almost preferred being back at the deli bar drinking beer, going to his ruined uncle's house to shoot up and crash. But over the weekend he'd had opportunity to remember the ugliness of that time, in fact to remember his uncle, a disgraced law professor and true drunk, and to remember his parents' and sister's heartbreak and his near-death experience. He knew he couldn't go back there. Besides, he was the do-gooder who had told his assistant about her husband. Also, he had counseled her husband to chill with the intern. So if it was his assistant calling, he was there.

He found the mute button. Butter said, "Hey, Lonnie," in an excited, high-pitched drawl. "Whatcha doing?" She sounded wonderful. He was glad it wasn't his assistant.

"Goodness. I'm ashamed to tell you." He closed one ear with his finger to shut out Jonah. "Did you call just now?"

"I'm sorry. I thought you might be showering and I didn't want you to know it was me who got you out all dripping, so I hung up. I've been in my garden. I've been up since six, Lonnie. I wrote a song and I put in some petunias."

Lonnie squinted at the TV screen. The picture cleared briefly on the product, an extra large, extra pink tongue undulating on a woman's wet thigh. "Creepy."

"Oh, yeah?"

"Not you."

"Why not me?"

"Because what you are is creamy. You are a cup of cocoa. Maybe you're pudding. Anyway, you are sweet, yet slightly salty to the taste, and altogether bad for me. You hike my blood pressure."

"Then you're forgiven. You want to hear my song?"

"I really don't know how you taste, exactly."

She sang to him in a breathy country-western voice, with a few saving soulful roller-coaster dips, about roadside wildflowers, bee pollen and glinting mica in the blacktop. He stared at the TV. Another woman, her image flickering in vertical waves, held two silver balls in her hand. They looked like the Chinese kind you see at flea markets or at Sharper Image, the musical balls you roll in one hand and are claimed to harmonize your whole body. He wondered what the TV woman would use them for; they seemed to be without much more than saliva. He felt too ignorant. He'd only had cable three weeks, and only because of Butter's insistence. He wondered what it would cost to have that channel straightened out.

Butter said, "That's it, brand new. Like me."

"Well it sounds familiar, like all hit songs should. I like it. But what's with the country flavor?"

"I'll pick you up at noon, if that's soon enough."

"I'll be my same old self." Then he wondered what old self he was talking about, still holding the phone to his ear after Butter hung up. Not a long time, but enough to make him chastise himself for spacing out. He thought, Well, Butter has definitely changed, so why not me, too?

The picture blinked to something altogether different, a weather map, it seemed. It was 9:00 according to the VCR clock. Lonnie scrolled up-channel. The *Today* show had gone off. Montel Williams was on in a band-collar shirt and a tight, scooped-neck vest. Everything about him seemed to match the curve of his bald head. He reminded Lonnie of the pencil sharpener he was supposed to be designing a box for.

"Up from slavery," he said to himself. He turned off

the TV, remembering how his father used to wake him up with that phrase. It became the household reveille. When Lonnie was a kid, his father would speak it gently as he sat on the edge of the bed and shook his shoulder. "Up from slavery, Sport." Later, during the drug days, the day nods and night comas, the wake-up got ruder— meaner. Even now Lonnie still said it, for the joke, and for not the joke. It kept him balanced in a way, happy and angry. Just so he knew where he was from and who he was, so he didn't forget anything.

He rolled off the sofa and went to his box drawings spread out on the glass dining table. The client wanted a sexy box, something to go with the sleek, round machine it would contain, which was almost an 8-ball with a single, silver-ringed hole. They wanted a standard square box with seductive art, a box that said, "Buy me, big boy." He'd done several drawings already, and sat now shading the circumference of one of the rendered pencil sharpeners, listening to Jonah tear up the backyard. He imagined dirt and root-torn weeds spinning in the tiller's wake. He thought about the TV tongue. Somebody had designed that. He guessed it had maybe two AA batteries in the thick end, powering the rotation of one or more s-bent wires to make the tongue lick. It was probably made of spongy rubber, like a Nerf toy, something soft and light. Or maybe covered with a thin, pliant vinyl. It was a big tongue, and it needed weight to be felt. The motor, he figured, provided that.

He was sketching tiny tongues around the pencil sharpener. He put tiny wings on them, like lewd little cupids. He added comma-sized saliva drops leaking off the tips. Next, he drew a woman's elegant hand cupping it. He leaned back in the chair and gazed up at the recessed ceiling light, imagined looking through to his bedroom upstairs where in the top drawer of the bureau was a vial containing three small rocks he'd bought from a kid at the apartments he still managed. He remembered from the old days the sweet, glassy taste and smell of the smoke and almost felt his head expand, like a helium balloon. When it went away, he looked back at the drawing. Maybe without the winged tongues, he thought.

He drew twelve versions, four with the elegant lady's hand reaching forward from a beautiful smiling face. The feminine hand, the feminine face with hand, each was good, and now he had to think about colors. He trotted up the spiral staircase to take the shower Butter had imagined. In the shower he tried to avoid imagining Butter.

Butter had blond hair. She'd told him she'd dyed it, but he had forgotten, and when she stood smiling in the doorway with a yellow pageboy, a white buttoned cardigan, and a short yellow skirt, his heart lightened in confusion until he realized who it was. Then he laughed. "Butter, you look great. I thought you were a beautiful stranger come to challenge me."

"Thank you, Lonnie. And what if I were a stranger? Would you have gone off with her and stood me up?"

"I would have been emboldened by my good fortune. I would have become arrogant and more flirtatious. I would have nibbled your delicious-looking neck." He stepped back to let her in. She brushed by smelling floral. He liked talking to Butter that way. She was the only woman who let him say those things.

"Lonnie, that's corn growing in your yard."

Jonah had turned on the sprinkler attached to the hose, its high arching spray ticking down on the glistening wet straw. "It's too early to tell."

He found her in the kitchen looking out the back door at Jonah, who had finished tilling and was now raking and gathering the dug-up weeds that had survived the death spray of two weeks before. The backyard was now waves of dirt, but there seemed to be too many clumps of live roots for Jonah, at his age, to bend for and bag by himself. Jonah was sixty-five. Root clumps littered the ground around him like small arthritic squid. He wore the all-khaki outfit he wore everyday—his janitor suit for his everyday job—plus the heavy-duty Black and Decker-style shoes and the khaki cap. He looked almost like an albino, an extra-white man. His cotton-white hair stuck out from the cap Harpo-like in silky tufts. His heavy, ropy, white-haired arms were sweat-slick and dirt-flecked, like his face.

Lonnie led Butter out to the edge of the deck. "What's it look like, Jonah?"

"Huh?" Jonah gazed up from where he squatted in the dirt. "Nothing. Almost through with this patch. Gotta plant seed. I need some more, though. And you ought to get another couple of hoses and sprinklers to keep the ground good and wet. You *ought* to have had the whole thing outfitted with underground sprinklers, like I told you. I could have done that for you, too."

He was looking past Lonnie to Butter, whose thin skirt was as negligent as a water-colored breeze. She didn't have great legs—the calves were too thin—but her skin was shiny and her thighs luscious and firm. Plus, Lonnie guessed he was thrown by her blond hair. He'd never met her, and he had a fetish for dark women, despite his more negative color bias, or maybe because of it. He was probably wondering where a woman that black got hair that straight and light. Once, when Lonnie came home from work, Jonah was waiting to tell him about a man he'd called the cops on. The man had been speeding down the street in a Plymouth that jumped the curb and stalled just two doors away. The man was black, Jonah said, but sick, it turned out, not drunk, in diabetic shock. So the guy's sister happens up behind the police to explain it all, and the sister is too fine, and Jonah believed that was his point, his inspiration for waiting on Lonnie at his door. Now, Lonnie decided to punish Jonah for the reason he'd called the cops. He suspected Jonah considered him O.K. for a black man because his skin was light, and that he had called the police because the diabetic was significantly dark. He looked to Butter and didn't introduce her. For a while he'd let Jonah suffer.

Jonah took off his gloves, stood up and slapped the gloves together like a seal. "I need that stuff today."

"Jonah, where have you been buying these supplies? Because this lady thinks we have corn growing out front."

"That's not corn. I guarantee you that's not corn, Lonnie. I got the first seeds from a buddy who hauls for a nursery. Got them wholesale. I gave you the receipt. That's just how grass looks at first."

Lonnie glanced again at Butter. She shrugged. She looked like a little girl in that skirt and sweater.

"You don't have to come with me. I see you got company. I need some more money, is what I'm getting at."

Butter said, "Lonnie, I need a rake. I need some plant steroids. I need to smell some garden chemicals."

Lonnie nodded to Jonah and he nodded back.

Butter sat in the middle while Jonah drove them in his old red truck. With her feet resting on the manifold hump her skirt rose higher. She wore black elastic sandals. Lonnie caught Jonah looking at her thighs. Her hands lay calmly clasped in her lap.

"There's a kangaroo," Butter said. She pointed to a blue house where something tall and nonhuman stood behind the screen door. They passed it rather fast but it did look a little kangarooish.

"That was what?" Jonah whipped his head to the side, too late.

"How can they keep it in a house?" She gazed back through the rear window, squinting.

"That had to be a person. It was eating something. See?" Lonnie tapped her on the shoulder. He mimicked taking a bite of something imaginary in his hand. "Eating a sandwich."

"No, no, it was scratching its face."

Jonah was looking in the rearview mirror. "It might have been like a elephant man."

"It was a big dog," Lonnie said, "like a Great Dane, standing up eating a sandwich."

Butter faced forward again. "The dog was behind the kangaroo, and it was drinking a soda pop."

Jonah looked worried. He turned onto the avenue and they drove awhile in silence. Butter tried the radio but it didn't work. The coat hanger sticking from the antenna nub spun. Lonnie put his arm across the back of the cracked vinyl seat and felt Butter jostle against him.

"I bought a red rubber skirt," Butter said, looking forward. They were passing under a traffic light just as it turned yellow. Lonnie thought, You can't draw that. You can't design a box like that. If I drew a truck under a yellow light, who's to say it just turned yellow? Maybe it was stuck on yellow. And right then, as Butter mentioned the red rubber skirt, Jonah hunched forward as if to show that he was not listening, to take himself out of the conversation lest she claim to see a turtle talking in a phone booth. His gray eyes grew paler with astonishment. Lonnie thought, Can you draw things happening that fast?

"How does it fit?"

"Hot and tight. I wore it to my class reunion."

"Oh, Butter," Lonnie said.

"Well, it was O.K. It was the house-party night. And Grim was with me. But this guy who used to be my friend came up and said, 'Damn, Phyllis, you got sexy.' You know, 'Geesh, thanks,' I said. Like I was a tooth before or something."

"You were not red rubber, I'm sure—Phyllis."

"Ball," Jonah mumbled.

"What?" Butter asked.

"Red rubber ball."

"No," Lonnie said.

"I'm just talking," Jonah said.

Butter made a funny scared face, pulling her bottom lip back. Lonnie petted her shoulder. "There were some balls on TV this morning," he said, partly to have fun with Jonah and partly to test Butter, she of the "hot and tight" red rubber. "Silver ones, palm-held, a sex aid apparently, but I don't quite get it."

Jonah kept his intent-on-driving posture. He and Butter said nothing. After awhile Elmer Fudd said, "Ben-Wa balls, for intimate stimuwation. Verwy contwolled. Verwy, verwy ancient." This came softly from Butter. Lonnie wanted to ask how she knew, and might have if not for Jonah. All of a sudden he didn't want her to expose herself to a stranger, or to him. Let her stay Elmer.

Jonah turned left onto the parkway, putting extra hand-over-hand action into being too busy driving to listen. Lonnie clutched Butter's shoulder to catch her from falling onto Jonah. Jonah had turned pink. He'd once shown Lonnie some magazines he had bought featuring interracial couples who wanted to swing. The pages showed black-and-white photographs of naked duos, their bodies slack and their faces hidden by black rectangles; they were posing in paneled, trailer living rooms, stark motel rooms, and on concrete, umbrella-shadowed patios. Jonah had seemed excited most by the local P.O. boxes for almost all the couples. If he could get himself a date, he'd said, he'd know what to do next.

"You know," Butter said, "I have an increased capacity for ecstasy."

She began to tell about something she and Grim had tried, something she had liked very much, involving the insertion and retrieval of grapes. Lonnie tried to change the subject: "Whoa, there's a goat driving a forklift." But she suggested trying chocolate-covered strawberries, and raspberries. She said that cherries were a cliché. So Lonnie offered, "Plums."

Jonah hunched himself so far onto the steering wheel it looked dangerous, as if he might climb over and crawl out the windshield and slide off the hood. The skin of his throat was deep red, the color surging up over his cheeks and into his temples.

Lonnie was still holding Butter, still palming her shoulder. She pushed up the sleeves of her sweater and unfastened the top buttons enough to expose cleavage and the white seam of a low-cut T-shirt. He had never noticed her cleavage before. She was enjoying making Lonnie and Jonah uncomfortable, Lonnie decided. They were her playthings. She was being *their* plaything, their fantasy, showing breast and thigh and talking dirty.

Fine, Lonnie thought. He looked at the silken skin on her arms, her black lashes and eyebrows, her brown skin framed by the precise blond cut. How did she look? Like fun? Like trouble? Ridiculous?

He described the tongue on TV, explained that he had been watching it when she called that morning, and said it might be good for some of that fruit-finding work she was fond of. Jonah started grinning, hugging the wheel and hopping in his seat. Butter asked how to get a tongue, how many speeds it had. Her legs seemed to lengthen as she leaned her knees toward Jonah and angled her heels toward Lonnie. Jonah swung into a bank parking lot and then back onto the street, for no apparent reason. "I don't know. What we gonna do?"

Lonnie laughed at him. "We're going to get grass seed. Why? What do you want to do?"

He shrugged. He shook his head, grinning. "I just want to get your yard done. I got me a date tonight. I want to get through and get cleaned up. Believe me, I got me a date."

Butter stared at him. "I believe you," and then she smiled at Lonnie. Her teeth were whiter than her sweater.

Butter and Lonnie waited in the truck at the supply store while Jonah went inside with Lonnie's credit card. Lonnie decided to let him load up a few things before going in to help him get it all out to the truck. He took his arm from around Butter and she slid over to the driver's side, her back against the door. She tilted her head out the window, arching her neck. "It's hot."

"Yeah. Who lit the furnace? We can get out."

"Not yet." She held out her hand to him. It was the hand he'd drawn all morning. He touched his fingertips to her.

"Your hand is on my box."

"What do you mean by that, Lonnie?"

"I'm not immune to you."

She smiled. She suddenly looked drunk, her eyes glassy and the smile insolent, not quite covering her gums and teeth. Maybe she looked sultry. "I could suck your lip and get all of you."

Lonnie fell back against the door, his hand over his heart, dramatically. But he said quietly, "Butter, what has happened?"

She closed her eyes awhile. When she opened them again, they were skittish; she couldn't look at him long. She seemed sad, age creeping into lines around her mouth, into the crease between her eyes. This all seemed inconsistent with her costumey blond hair.

"I know I'm shocking." She gazed down at her elegant fingers. Her head lolled to each side, her eyes closed. She put her hands to her breasts, squeezed, dropped her hands to her lap like shot birds. "I'm not used to myself." She looked steadily at him now, spread her big eyes open wider with her fingertips. "I've been, like, locked."

"You're, like, not now."

"Yes. Not since I kissed Kenny Pantu."

"Who?"

"Kenuichio Pantu, the dancer. When I was volunteering for the dance festival, remember?" She relaxed the extra-big eye pose to blink. Then she held them open again.

"The goatee guy?" Lonnie did remember. Butter and some of her friends had taken free workshops with some of the dance troupes. He'd met Pantu at a party she'd told him about, and he saw him a few times afterward, even went to a performance. But what he remembered most about that party was a young woman who complained about her roommate's cats. She sat on the floor, and Lonnie watched fleas leap around on her legs.

"He had on all black," Butter said.

"He was all cliché."

"No he wasn't. Was he?"

"He was O.K. You needn't tell me anything, Butter. I don't want you to."

"Well, I told Grim. I was the one who picked up Kenny at the airport. We stopped on the roadside because he wanted a close-up view of the color flashing by us in the woods. We hiked up a hill and he kissed me in those wildflowers. My song." She winked.

"All right. You had fun and you got a song out of it.

Nothing altogether wrong with that. Nothing to tell Grim about, was it?"

"The point is, I kissed him back, and he was touching me, and I was thinking of you."

"Oh, yuck, Butter."

"Fuck you, Lonnie."

"Fuck you, too. I mean, what the hell are you doing, now of all times?" He couldn't manage any more words. He was thinking "thank you" and feeling betrayed.

She opened the truck door, hopped out, stood on the pavement awhile, got back in. She swung the door in and out. "I'm not immune to you, too, Lonnie. I don't know when you're playing and when you're serious with me. I mean, I know you're playing, but you're serious, too, right?"

"Oh, hell, Butter. You know what I'm trying to do, don't you? Protect me, protect you?"

"Come on, now. I mean, you're safe with me." She paused. "You're not...clinical, are you?"

"What? No. Not that, at least." Right then he wanted to be in Home Depot looking for Jonah among the bags of potting soil, wandering aisles of metal snippers and hacksaws and nails. He'd rather have confronted his boss with his secret wife than finally to be really in love with Butter. After her admission to being other than committed to Grim, to being, in essence, fed up with her life, he told her to close the truck door. He told her what she didn't know about him, about the variety of drugs and the moral adventures thereof, how he had OD'd and died, how his father found him slumped on the toilet surrounded by wallpaper of gold foil butterflies-and-fireworks and beat the crap out of him, so that by the time the paramedics arrived he had a broken nose, black eyes, a bruised chest and bleeding lips, with his dad ludicrously screaming "Up from slavery," no doubt seeing his no-good brother, Lonnie's ruined uncle, who'd thrown away a law career on liquor and sexual harassment of his law students. Lonnie had made his dad, the steady dentist, flip out trying to save his life. He'd made his mother and sister scared of him. He stopped with the drugs right then—no more —with a month of first-class professional emotional counseling, plus his own amateur treatment. But since then he'd been too ashamed to have much contact with his family, whom he'd been blaming for his debauchery before. And to take what Butter was offering felt somehow damaging and wrong, because just when he had trained himself to resist, she had decided to say yes, and for him to say yes now would confuse or kill him and maybe sabotage her. He had the impression she might do anything he asked, and he was afraid of what he might ask. Let's see how long we can live without food. Let's go to the courthouse naked. Let's not go to work. Let's get bigger fruit. Let's get dogs. Let's see how much money you can make. Let's put this syringe in your head. Let's see how long we can hold this hose. Let's put on each other's skin. He was not exactly her guy, and he told her.

"Anyway, what about Grim?"

"Grim hates you."

"Jesus, Butter. Grim doesn't hate me."

"Yes, he does. I think. Don't ask me why."

"All right. I can't take this. It's too hot."

"Fine. Ask me why. He disapproves of you, then.

You're a privileged, irresponsible narcissist. You're a self-indulgent baby."

He got out of the truck and headed into the gardening area. It was steaming in there. They had a mist system spraying the philodendrons and roses. He took a turn toward deeper shade and for a while was in a maze of hanging, dripping ferns and orchids, and huge orange-blooming birds-of-paradise. Giant, pink-speckled caladiums brushed his leg, like vegetable tongues. That was interesting—funny—how the tongue image was following him around today. Pretty soon all the plants looked like tongues, and he started to believe they were holding things to say about him, or were about to lick him away to nothing—consume him. The air was cool but so thick and the smell so earthen he felt like he was breathing dirt. He took deep breaths and held them.

He didn't really want to find Jonah but wanted to go home. His own yard smelled like this, and he would be much more comfortable there. He stopped and held his breath and imagined taking a nap, dreaming. He'd dream about a hurricane and an ocean-green sky. He'd dream about wind. Every red-faced Jonah, woosh. Every slum apartment, swoosh. Every well-kept lawn, every chunk of crack, every box, every boss, every drug and every addict, every helpless parent and child, every wagging tongue, every man, woman, Butter, him, gone.

Then he opened his eyes, and realized where he'd gotten the ocean-green sky; the light in there was underwater light, through a translucent green corrugated roof. He wove his way out of the foliage and into the cavernous store. He wandered up and down aisles of rakes and weed killers, chicken wire and padlocks, paint and ax handles, until he saw Jonah pulling a tangerine-colored cart piled high with twenty-pound bags of seed. Jonah was a few aisles away, passing under an orange banner that read "Electrical." Lonnie tried to catch up with him, but was blocked by a little white hydraulic truck that was lifting a man up to some cabinets near the ceiling. He stood in front of a display of whirling fans. Hey, wind, he thought. He put his face to one with clear blue blades and hummed. He said into the fan, "Hi. My name is Lonnie Welcome, and I'm trapped in a world of heavy merchandise." His voice trembled spastically, and he chuckled, thinking he sounded almost as unsteady during his dramatic confession to Butter.

Butter came out of an aisle on the other side of the hydraulic truck. She wasn't wearing her sweater. Her white T-shirt was tiny, tummy-bearing, and made of acetate. It had a picture of a red cat's face on the front under the words "Killer Pussy." She waved. Jonah followed her out of the aisle, pulling the cart full of seed. He waved. "Where you been?" he said, nodding his head and cutting his eyes at Butter's chest.

"Hey," Lonnie said into the fan, waving back, his voice quavering. "Heyyyyyyy."

Finally, they got home, and Jonah went back to work on the yard, unloading the bags of seed and pushing them round back in the wheelbarrow. Butter began pulling on Lonnie's belt, and he thought O.K., looks like I'm doing this. He wanted to but he didn't want to seem like it. That she could be any way she chose was awfully irresistible. It seemed like a freedom he could have, if he could have her. A convenient logic, he knew. He resisted by backing to the foot of the stairs so she could pull him up to the bedroom. But once there, after she unbuttoned his shirt, she began to apologize for her breasts. "They are not what they appear."

"Oh?"

"I'm wearing a bra."

"I know that."

She turned toward the window that overlooked the backyard. She peeled off her little shirt and stood looking out the window at the tops of trees and neighbors' houses. She didn't move. He thought perhaps he should unhook her bra, which was black, but there was no clasp in the back.

"You won't like them. They're not beautiful. One is smaller than the other."

"I don't care. How small is the big one?"

She turned quickly and leapt on him, knocking him onto the bed. Her knees dug into his ribs, and she fell over and clamped his chest in a scissor lock. "Try to get out."

He couldn't quite breathe. She had knocked the breath out of him and wasn't letting him get it back. He pinched the flesh of her leg, and she unhooked her ankles but scrambled up to his head and locked her knees to his ears. "How's this?"

Suddenly he caught a breath and pinched her again, and when she relaxed her squeeze, he rolled over on his stomach to calm himself. She sat on his back, her knees on his shoulders, and put her mouth to his ear. "You didn't know I could wrestle, did you? Grim doesn't like it. He's afraid he'll hurt me."

She bounced on him and dropped her bra onto the side of his face. Then she was tugging his pants off. "You're not supposed to pinch," she said as she yanked. "You can spank, maybe, but not pinch."

Lonnie turned over, expecting her to be ready to hit him or jump on him. But she was just standing there holding his pants, wearing only the short, thin skirt and breathing hard. She was smiling gleefully, strands of her new hair sticking out, her chest like glistening brown velvet.

She threw herself onto Lonnie again, her breasts—seeming ample and equal—snapping his chest. They tussled off the rest of their clothes, half wrestling and half trying to consummate their peculiar affection. They tried all sorts of ways to hold onto each other. They were sweaty in the afternoon heat, and found each other incredibly sweet.

Afterwards, lying there, Butter said, "Look." Her thigh was over his in such a way that the contrast in color was startling. "We've made the yin-yang symbol. You're a pale-assed dude."

"Yeah. So what?"

"Don't be angry."

"I'm not." But he was, though not at her really. He didn't need her making them into a symbol of anything just then. He was already feeling guilty, as if he had done something irrevocable, immutable, karmic. He was thinking about Grim's hating him, which was startling again. He was wondering whether or not Butter and he could leave each other alone, whether he'd be able to leave her alone. He hadn't believed he could hurt Grim. But he suspected he had hurt himself, and was yet to feel the pain.

Jonah was outside showering the yard with seed and yellow straw. Lonnie could hear it and smell it through the open window. What had Jonah heard, he wondered. Being in love with Butter seemed insane. Grim was likely to try some damage. He worried that Butter was as dangerous and pleasant as the drugs. She offered their paradox; he wasn't supposed to have what he wanted, and he didn't want what he had, no matter how badly he needed it. It was precisely the kind of mess that scared him. Right now he wanted a drink.

Butter snuggled against him and whispered, "Lonnie, what's it like to be dead?"

He held her tighter. He pulled the sheet over them. He never wanted to let her go. "For me there was no bright light, unless I was too stoned to notice."

"The welcoming calm?"

"That might have been the drug."

"Desire?"

"I don't know. A little bit."

"Good," she said into his neck.

It lasted two months, and Butter called him a coward when he backed out. "I can't. It's not me." She was angry, but several months later she was back with Grim. Lonnie ordered the tongue for her, kept it in the plain brown box in his bedroom. He never opened it, as he never opened the vial of crack he bought from the boy at the apartments. He thought of sending the box to his father with a note reading, "I'm speechless," maybe send the vial along, too. But he doubted his dad would think it was a joke, or an apology; his mother would be insulted, and, with all the talk that would follow, his sister would find out and be revulsed, because it was complicated and she was still too young to understand.

Why They Named
the Baby Lake

LAURA WILSON WAS the first to greet them, just as Rita was finishing recombing her newly bobbed hair in the car's courtesy mirror. Mayes recognized Laura from photographs she had sent during the last twenty-two months. He supposed she knew him and Rita from their photographs, though he couldn't imagine she expected some other black couple would come rolling up for a Sunday visit by mistake. "You made it," she yelled from the trailer door as Mayes and Rita got out of the car. It had been an hour-and-forty-minute drive.

Laura's blond hair rose artificially high on the top of her head and fanned out less dramatically as it draped to her shoulders. She had that strange mixture of bigness and boniness—a tall, wide skinny woman. She wore white shorts and a sleeveless white blouse with yellow flowers embroidered on the collar. A long cigarette burned in her pink-nail fingers as her outstretched arms closed in a rocking embrace around Rita.

Then she turned to Mayes. Her cheek felt cool, moist and thin. The smoke of her cigarette stung his nostrils and made him bitterly nostalgic for when he used to smoke. She pulled back, smiling broadly, showing big glossy teeth and brown eyes.

"Come on. Paul and Lake are inside." But it was clear she was excited to be in the sun finally meeting her friend Rita, with whom she had been bonding on the phone for nearly two years, since the day her husband, Paul, delivered living-room tables to Mayes's and Rita's house and left his wallet in the kitchen after lunch. He'd been showing Rita his family's pictures. Rita had been telling him her life's story. Her life had gotten more complicated since then, with the kidnapping. But she had told Laura all about that. Besides, that was over now, almost—plea-bargained. Suspended sentence. Suspended wonder. Suspended truth.

"You're so pretty," Laura sang to Rita, holding on to Rita's forearms.

"Oh, you sweetie," Rita sang back. "Look at you. Look at us."

They were dressed nearly alike. Rita's shorts and sleeveless blouse were sky-blue with white flowers stitched

delicately along the shirt buttons. She wore blue sandals—she'd painted her toenails dark red in the car—and
Laura wore white sandals with laces that tied around her
ankles.

"You're sisters."

"Yes we are." They giggled at Mayes, and seemed to
blush with pleasure and embarrassment at each other's
indulgent girlishness.

Mayes stood in the yard's red dirt with his hands in his
pockets, waiting to follow them up the trailer's stoop. It
was good to see Rita happy, but he had never wanted to
come out for this visit. He didn't know these people and
he wasn't sure Rita knew them all that well, though he
did marvel at how she and Laura had become friends over
long-distance, without ever having seen each other. He
was shy about Paul. He didn't like feeling forced to be
pals with someone he'd never even spoken to. He imagined an afternoon of strain trying to talk about cars or
cockfighting, whatever Paul was into. He glanced about
and didn't see any chickens, no rooster cages, not much
other than the red-dirt road they had driven in on and
the woods bordering it. He looked again at the salmon-
colored Lincoln and the iridescent-blue Firebird parked
headlight-to-headlight under an oak tree off to the right.
They were the landmarks to look for among the few trail-
ers along the road. They gleamed through a thin layer
of dust in the sunlight that dropped through the tree
branches. He could go in and fake some talk about pistons
and torque, he thought. Maybe ask about the paint jobs.

Paul sat in an armchair watching preseason pro football on a big color TV. Their granddaughter, Lake, was

bouncing on the pink toy car Rita and Mayes had sent for her first birthday four months before. She slapped down on the red horn in the middle of the steering wheel when she saw them come in, her squealing red mouth wet with happiness.

"She's done got so she can ride that thing," Paul said, standing. He shook Mayes's hand. Rita hugged him and kissed his lips.

"How's grandpa?" she asked. "You look like a good ole grandpa."

"Oh, he is," Laura said. "He loves that little girl to death."

Mayes cut in, "Well, I can see why." He lifted Lake up from her car. She had the soft, satisfying heft that tempted him to pick up all babies. His and Rita's girls were bigger, the younger ones barely scoopable. Lake looked at him wide-eyed, and then leaned out to be taken by Rita.

"Man," Mayes said to Paul, "I can't even fool a one-year-old."

"Don't worry about it. Take a load off."

He sat on the plaid sofa next to Paul's armchair. On the wall behind the television set stretched a row of framed 8 × 10 portraits, each with a different fake Sears-type backdrop. Mayes had seen a few of them before, in 5 × 7 versions Laura had mailed to them. Most were of their daughter Dee, Lake's mother, whose recent running away was the reason Rita chose now, finally, to visit. She was a heavy young girl with long permed brown hair and thickly mascaraed eyes. In those pictures she was nowhere near the glamour she was striving for.

Mayes was about ready for a beer, but Paul wasn't

drinking one, so he didn't know whether they kept any in the house. Rita had carried Lake to the other end of the long room, where a flowery, antique-looking love seat and two ottomans flanked a round, ornate coffee table, set on a blue, white-fringed rug. She sat on the love seat and balanced Lake on her knee while Laura perched on an ottoman and slipped a pacifier into the baby's mouth. "This is your aunt Rita," Laura kept saying. "Yes, it is."

"What's the score?" Mayes asked.

"Nothing much. I'm just half paying attention. You found us all right?"

Mayes nodded and stared at the TV, the volume down low. There didn't seem much to do. Neither of them seemed to like the company of other men much. Paul had his elbows propped on the high padded arms of the chair. He had the look of a thoughtful man, and that worried Mayes. He might decide to give his views on race relations, as a lot of white people liked to do. Mayes was waiting for his affirmative-action ideas, or his account of some illuminating experience with a black person he worked with. For Rita's sake, Mayes was going to have to be polite about it, as he usually was anyway, such as when he was at a conference and somebody wanted to know if, "as an African-American," he had an advantage or a disadvantage on his job. This was a reason Mayes had not wanted to spend a summer Sunday here, but he had kept that to himself. Rita would have just driven by herself and been madder at him than usual. As it was, they'd had a kind of argument in the car about how generous she was with strangers. The argument had made him feel deficient.

So right now it was his job to be chummy. The only

questions that came to mind were for things Mayes already knew about Paul, and asking them would be patronizing, fraudulent. *What do you do for a living? Haul furniture for a factory, on the road for weeks at a time trucking up and down the East Coast?* Rita had told Mayes all about it, the way she and Laura had probably told Paul about Mayes —that he worked for a company that did low-temperature research, traveled a little bit sometimes, came home, went to bed, got up and started again.

"So I hear you're a doctor, or scientist, or something."

"Yeah, both. I freeze shit."

"What the hell good is froze shit?"

"Not actual shit. But everything else. Metal, gases, diamonds."

"I know you don't freeze actual shit. At least I didn't *think* you did. I was joking."

"Oh. O.K." Mayes watched the football game. A player on the field was down, attended to by trainers. "We're reaching some extra-low temps, though. Maybe some Russian or German is reaching similar numbers. There will be some claims, I'm sure."

"The Russians, I believe, can't reach nothing much these days. And if you ain't careful the Japanese will up and steal and copy whatever something you froze good enough."

Mayes chuckled a little, assuming Paul was still joking. He was surprised to find the guy so jovial.

Paul had stopped hauling four months ago, because of heart surgery. Doctors used an artery in his leg to replace a collapsed one in his heart. Lately he was trying to decide whether or not to retire on disability or to go back for two more years for full benefits. The trailer was filled with factory-irregular furniture, but that wasn't what he missed about the work. Laura told Rita that sometimes he stood out in the road ruts and just stared.

Mayes knew things that even Paul didn't know, such as Laura's secret request for money when Paul was in the hospital. Rita mailed a check for $300. Mayes knew that Laura had a boyfriend with whom she was planning to leave until Paul got sick, and that, according to Rita, she didn't know what she would do now that he was better and now that Dee had left them the baby. She was fed up with this trailer and this living way out yonder.

Mayes felt sorry for him. He seemed a nice, mild guy, though he had faint, short eyelashes that made his pale-blue eyes look lidless. His gaze was unnerving unless he smiled, in which case he appeared too surprised. He was sixty-four, some eight or ten years older than Mayes and Rita, twelve years older than Laura. He was average height, but his narrow shoulders compressed him, and his face and feet were small. It seemed he probably had trouble finding grown-up shoes to fit. He wore loose, beige rubber-soled slip-ons, the kind in Wal-Mart bins linked by a stubborn plastic string.

The team couldn't move the ball, and after a punt and no return Mayes mentioned the split-barrel grill outside under a shade tree. "Is that how we're eating?"

"Partly. Laura likes it. I can't eat what I used to. There's stuff already cooked in the kitchen." He flicked off the TV with the remote control. "This game is ugly. Sunday takes forever; you know what I mean?" He spit something off the tip of his tongue and tossed a foam yellow ball over at Lake.

"Hey," Laura said. "You guys want to play, go outside."

"Let's look around," he said to Mayes, getting up.

Mayes followed him to the kitchen, where a counter separated the sink and avocado appliances from a dinette table, set with glazed red plastic plates and a silk flower centerpiece. Paul flipped open a cooler on the countertop. "Help yourself."

"Thanks." Mayes fished around in the ice among ginger ales and orange drinks until he came up with something grape flavored. No beer. Paul went out the back door onto a deck, which was a work in progress, or renovation. What Mayes took to be streaks of sunlight were planks of fresh wood laid down among the original, gray-painted decking. The sky had grown dull. A new rail was partially up. The old, replaced lumber was piled on the ground off to the side.

"Now that the baby's walking, I have to safen it up out here."

"You're doing it yourself?"

"It's exercise."

They sat down on the step and looked out on two or more acres of wild terrain, much of it a crater of brush and trees backed in the distance by forest. A crooked path led through stiff, dry-looking brush toward another old wooden platform. Mayes pointed his drink can at it.

"That's the pier. I built it so I could go fishing. Might as well just let that rot where it will."

"Fishing where? There used to be water out there?"

"That's why I bought out here. So I could come home after my runs and wet a hook. It was real pretty. But then it dried up."

"Damn. That's pretty cruel."

"That ain't nothing." He unfastened two of his shirt buttons to show Mayes the top of his surgery scar. It looked like a fat red worm half buried in his chest.

"You survived that?" Mayes raised his eyebrows.

"Yeah."

"You must be one tough son-of-a-gun."

"That's what I hear." He fastened the shirt again. "Anyway, you know Dee named the baby Lake to sort of give it back to me."

"It's a pretty name," Mayes said. He sipped his grape soda. A couple of birds, hawks probably, sailed slowly over the trees. Mayes felt a relief not to be drinking beer. It was good to sit out here, on raw wood, and look at the sky. Maybe he should stop drinking altogether, the way he had stopped smoking. Just stop, as he had promised the people at A.A. Self-improve.

"Have you heard from her?"

"Dee? She's got way out to Colorado." Paul ran his hand through his thin hair, and looked at his fingers. "She called last night. Said she's gonna get a job and go to school. Hell, I been trying to get her to do that here. But she'd rather be with that boy she went off with."

"You'd think she'd like it right here in nowhere," Mayes said, sounding more snide that he intended. So he said, "She went off with Lake's father?"

"No, man. We don't know where *he* is. This is some kid who showed up at the bowling alley with a brand-new Mustang. Dee likes Mustangs, now. Meanwhile, I'm still paying on that Firebird I got for her out front."

"I'm a Chevy man, myself."

"I heard."

A burst of laughter sounded from inside. That's good, Mayes thought. That's what they were here for. Laura had been in tears a lot on the phone with Rita, crying over selfish teenage Dee; crying over Lake, who had been having one ear infection after another, and then asthma; crying over Paul, who was making her feel trapped, who never showed her any attention until his heart made him stay home, until it was too late. Anyway, he was the one getting the attention. She had to make sure he took his medicine, make sure he ate right, make sure he stayed dumb about her boyfriend.

Paul shut the door. He put his hand on Mayes's shoulder and strode off the deck onto the path. Mayes hesitated but Paul didn't look back, so he took a big swig of the drink and pushed off behind him.

It was a narrow path of matted grass over intermittent loose and buried rocks. Paul moved fast. His reddened heels slipped in and out of his shoes. As he swung his arms, his truck-steering, furniture-lifting muscles stretched the weave of his tan knit shirt. Mosquitos swarmed around his neck just below the neatly trimmed hairline. Mayes supposed he'd gotten the fresh haircut just for him and Rita, which Mayes regarded as a courtesy. But he wished Paul could be mindful that Mayes was a city boy, wearing sandals and shorts. He hadn't been out in the rough in years, not since *he* had lived in the country, growing up. Sharp weeds stung his legs, and he kept slapping himself because of the mosquitos.

Mayes thought they were headed for the pier, but Paul turned right, through a brief clearing that led into the forest. They came to another clearing and a cabin, all

canopied by towering pine trees whose fallen needles cush-
ioned the ground. It was a fishing cabin, something Paul
must have built when the lake was full. A couple of ragged, straw-bottomed chairs tilted forward against the
porch rail. A limp, dingy string hammock bowed between
two thick trees off to the left.

Paul unpadlocked the front door. The one rough room
had a Formica-topped table with mildewed yellow direc-
tor's chairs tucked up neatly to it. A full-sized refrigerator
stood against the kitchen-area wall. On the counter by a
sink was a square black boom box, and on the shelves
were magazines, Windex, Liquid Wrench, aerosol cans,
batteries, small jars, rocks, and odd-shaped pieces of wood.
A few decent-sized snake skins decorated another wall,
behind a sofa covered in a light green sheet.

"I shot those snakes. This was a good ole drinking cabin
after the lake disappeared, but now I done quit drinking.
People think that's because of my bum heart."

"It's not?"

"No. I got worried that if I didn't do it when I did I
was gonna have to find Jesus to quit, and I didn't want
to have to go around thanking the Lord, being an example, like your black musicians on those award shows."

Mayes laughed. "White musicians don't do that, do
they?"

"Just the Jesus-freak ones, I guess."

Paul sprayed the counter with Windex and began wip-
ing it down with a dish cloth. From where Mayes stood,
in the middle of the room, the cabin windows looked like
cellophane, the views outside distorted.

"You want to hear something funny? Sometimes, late

at night, I lay in bed looking at the ceiling, listening for Lake, and I think that the doctors delivered me of evil. I feel so blessed to be alive. I imagine that's what they secretly did when they went in there. I get out my own stethoscope and I listen to my heart. But, you know, that stubborn heartbeat, it's mind-numbing. Is that how it's supposed to sound? So maybe they botched it, I think. Such times I feel like I don't want this thing. It keeps up too steady a beat and I'm not doing nothing, I don't go nowhere. Like it's mocking me."

"You're having a nightmare. You should take a sleeping pill."

Paul gazed up at Mayes. 'I'll tell you something else I quit. I quit saying nigger."

Oh, shit, Mayes thought. 'No kidding." He felt small supports in his own chest weaken. He stiffened, tried to keep his face straight.

"I wonder if Laura's even noticed." He grinned down at the counter he was scrubbing, as if he had sneaked home a footstool he was waiting for her to notice. "She used to get on me about it. I hadn't said it in months until just then. Before now, I never told anybody I stopped."

"Well, why are you telling me? Why don't you go tell some white people?" He could hardly believe he was in this conversation. He caught himself rubbing and scratching the back of his hand, his knuckles, where he'd been bitten.

"It wouldn't make them no difference, I don't think. I figured it'd make a difference to you."

"You did, huh?"

He shrugged, sprayed more of the counter, and wiped

some more. "I figure you're the one who don't want me to say it. You meaning black people. So I won't. It's partly because of your wife."

"I doubt that."

"She's extra special. *You* ought to know. Coming through that kidnap like she done. Caring about me and Laura like she does. Me and Laura both love Rita. I just wouldn't want to hurt her feelings in particular. It's like when your Miss America, Vanessa Williams, had those naked pictures in the magazines. I didn't look at them because I knew she didn't want me to. Did you look at them?"

"Yeah, I saw them."

"Well, you shouldn't have." He shook his finger at Mayes.

"But there's another thing. See, black people think they got all the trouble. They think because white people don't like them, call them that word, then that's the cause of their trouble. Well, that's trouble all right, but white people have got trouble, too." He cocked his head to the side, rubbing hard on the counter, the tip of his tongue poking out. "Get rid of that word and then blacks can appreciate white people's problems."

"So white people own and control *all* the problems, you're saying. That's a good one. That might even be true."

"I'm saying that since white people can't know what it's like to be black, we got to stop *making* ya'll be black, so you can see what it's like to be white. To just be human."

"Look, *ya'll* need to just be human." Mayes stopped

himself. He despised this. He had a mean feeling about
Rita sitting in the house and having no idea, or care, about
what was happening out here. But it struck him that he
didn't know what she was doing. Offering Laura what
she needed, he supposed. Getting warm emotional nour-
ishment herself, he guessed.

He opened the refrigerator. Three plastic gallon jugs of
water glowed gray-white on the metal racks. A shriveled
box of baking soda seemed stuck to the back. He breathed
in the chilled vapor awhile. "Maybe we ought to talk
about something else, or go on back and worry about the
grill."

Paul didn't respond. He put up the glass cleaner and
rinsed and folded the cloth. Mayes walked to the back of
the room and peered out the window at a thick tangle of
trees right up on the cabin wall. They hadn't even eaten,
yet. There were hours before he could say to Rita, We'd
better get home.

A mosquito zinged his ear and he swatted himself. He
remembered the argument he and Rita had on the way.
She teased him, called him a racist, and he overreacted.
Maybe she wasn't teasing. He almost shouted at her. He
said, "Look, I have *always* been an integrationist. I *believe*
in the brotherhood of man. I'm just tired of the bullshit,
that's all. It's old. *I'm* old. This effort—I want out of it,
that's all."

Paul came up and handed him a green can of insect
repellent. He cradled a large metal stongbox under his
arm. "There's something inside here." He took it to the
sofa and unlocked it.

He lifted out folded sheets of paper bound in rubber

bands, and a box of audiocassettes. Mayes sprayed repellent on his arms and legs, rubbed it on his neck, while Paul hunched over and looked at what was written on one of the pages. The bites, where Mayes had scratched them, burned.

"These are photocopies of love letters." Paul held out a bundle. "Evidence. What I do is work hard, see. This is part of my work. The doctors say I had at least two heart attacks some months before I got sick enough to get operated on. I say tell me about it." He fanned another folded paper. "This is my will, which I have to change. I've got my snake pistol in here, some other stuff." He handed Mayes a stack of color snapshots. "You can look at these."

Mayes snatched the pictures, disliking the intimacy Paul seemed to believe he had created. They were of Laura in states of gradual undress. The top one showed her standing in the living room in a yellow pants suit. The next showed her in the pants and her bra, the shirt over her arm. Then, no pants. He gave them back.

"She wouldn't mind. We were gonna make a scrapbook for our real old age, but something happened. We got mad at each other. There's some of both of us in there."

"No thanks."

"We're not doing nothing. Just posing."

"Whatever."

"We had a lot of fun back then." He set the pictures aside. "It don't matter now."

He got up and slipped one of the cassette tapes into the boom box. They listened to loud hiss until Laura began talking. Mayes couldn't understand all she was saying, and then a man's voice began. Paul had recorded one of her rendezvous. Soon there were chuckles and sighs.

"That was in my Lincoln. A recorder's under the dash. Most of these are phone tapes. So mostly it's just talk."

He changed tapes and fast-forwarded to the place he wanted. The man said, "What if he doesn't make it?" And Laura answered, "I don't know. This is all too much." She paused awhile. "It wouldn't be all bad." And the man said, "No. Something good could come of it." And Laura said, "Yes. I wouldn't have to leave him. I wouldn't have to hurt him. He wouldn't have to know."

Paul stopped the tape. "Well, I do know. What they don't know is me." He took out the cassette. "Did you know?"

Mayes took a deep breath. "I guess not."

Paul lowered his head with a dim smile. "You're lying."

"Is that on the tapes, too?"

"Afraid so. There's talk about Rita and all, who could be happier herself, by the way. She says we all deserve better than we get. That's what she says according to Laura, on one of these tapes here. She's a kind person. So you got better than you deserve. Now, you don't have no problems, do you, when you think about mine?"

"What do you mean, she could be happier?"

He gave a short laugh. "At least she don't wish you was dead. But that's O.K. Everything and everybody's gonna die. Everything's almost gone already."

He rested against the counter, his arms folded. Then he turned and opened a closet beside the refrigerator. He pulled out a rifle. It had a telescopic sight on it. "I want you to understand me."

"You're not crazy, are you?"

"Hey, now that would be a problem, wouldn't it?"

He began loading the rifle with cartridges from one of the boxes on the shelf.

Mayes looked inside the strongbox for the pistol Paul had mentioned. "You plan to shoot something?"

"It's wrapped in that towel," Paul said.

Mayes lifted out the heavy white towel from under a stack of envelopes. He unwrapped a smooth, wooden-handled, double-barreled pistol—a kind of sawed-off shotgun.

"You know what, Paul? You got the blues. You got one of those country-western blues. The fish ain't bitin' 'cause the lake done dried. Your wife is mad 'cause she thinks you shoulda died. Put a tune to it. It's a bad time to be thinking about guns."

"Ever seen one of those?"

Mayes shook his head.

"Let me load it for you." He stepped over and gave Mayes the rifle. He broke open the pistol and dropped in two shells, then snapped it shut. He replaced the cassettes and papers in the strongbox and put them away in the closet.

"Let's go." He stared at Mayes, the bones of his face sharp under his pale skin. "Ready?"

"Yeah."

"I want you to understand *me*."

They took a different path through the woods. They didn't come right out into the clearing. Paul held the pistol beside his leg, and Mayes carried the rifle over his shoulder, the way he thought was safe. Mayes thought, This guy has a death wish, and the insanity of people angered him. He thought, You ignorant son of a bitch, talking to me about Rita's dissatisfaction. He thought, You self-centered sneaky son of a bitch. Mayes grew mad at him for being a stupid white man. He thought about all the problems black people did have because of people like Paul. He thought about how messed up some black people were, enslaved, manipulated, taken away from themselves, how they were forced to think about white people all the damn time. It's a black thing, Mayes thought, derisively, disgusted with himself; he hated it when people said that.

Then, oddly, he had a sensation he hadn't felt since he was a kid, when he used to hike through the woods with his friends. He used to imagine that he entered another dimension, an alternate world, one similar to the other one because the woods stayed the same. But his friends would disappear and he would be walking alone, and he would panic because it seemed too real, as if it could happen, had happened, and he'd have to jump on his friends and wrestle to get securely back in the world, or just hit one of them on the shoulder.

"Paul."

"What?"

"Nothing." Mayes watched his red heels slipping in and out of his shoes. "Paul, where're we going? What are we doing?"

Paul didn't say anything, and Mayes felt that panic. He watched Paul's head. He listened to their footsteps and the noisy whisk of Paul's new slack jeans. He thought, I could blow your head off; that would put me in the world.

They came out of the woods onto the warped, bleached

pier. Mayes was surprised to find himself there, so in the open. The air felt cooler, a high, light gray covering the sun. They stood side by side holding the guns. They gazed down into the deep expanse of gnarled brush, weeds, pine trees and maples. Loose items of trash littered the slope —flattened cans and paper cups, a faded orange detergent box, a twisted T-shirt. "What I do is come out here and shoot. This is where I kill snakes and whatever."

Mayes was annoyed at the triteness. "Do you know about Sigmund Freud and Karl Jung?"

Paul's pale eyes looked at Mayes blankly. "I heard of them." He held the long-barreled pistol at his hip with two hands and fired. The boom echoed in the dry lake cavern and a bush popped with buckshot. "They ain't got nothing to do with this."

Mayes started to explain what he knew about all these symbols—the creeping snakes, the absent lake, this large hole Paul shot into, the guns, his vacant, vacating women. But he decided not to bother. What's a symbol to somebody who doesn't care about it, who won't or can't read it? And he wondered what was going on that he was missing? Because, on the other hand, these were not symbols; there was nothing out here at all.

Mayes turned and saw Laura and Rita standing back at the trailer on the deck, Laura holding Lake. She cuddled the baby's head to her chest, her hand over the child's ear. Rita broadly waved them in.

Mayes recalled the image of Laura in the photos, in her underwear. He remembered his cheek against hers. He thought about her on the tapes, her whispers and sighs. He imagined Dee in Colorado, across the country and thinking only of having somebody desire her. And he looked at Rita in the distance—urbane, prim and, according to Paul, perfect. He wondered what really she had in common with them, how she and Laura could be such friends. He didn't understand them. He didn't understand Paul. He didn't understand anybody or anything, he decided.

"Shoot something," Paul said. "Then we'll go light the fire."

Something glinted by a fallen splintered tree about sixty yards center. It had been flickering at him. That was curious because the sun had not come back out, and Mayes thought he shouldn't even be seeing it. He wildly imagined the baby waddling out here and being charmed by it, and falling off the pier, killing herself trying to get it. It might have been a drink can, a piece of glass, a partially hidden hubcap, but where was the light coming from?

He tried to imagine what Rita was thinking. Was she feeling frightened, entertained, or disgusted with him out here firing guns with Paul? She should be out here, he thought. Break them out of the cliché, and identify that light.

"Paul. What is that out there?"

Paul gave Mayes his lidless look and then added the surprised, idiotic smile. "That's yours."

Mayes raised the rifle and tried to steady the glint in its magnifying sight. What's mine? he asked himself. It was a strange time to feel helpless, holding a gun, for some reason wanting Paul to respect him, wanting Rita to love him, wanting to settle some wavering about himself.

"This world," he said, aloud, as if to himself, but to Paul, too. He aimed, holding the light bright on his eye, urging, Whatever it is, just let me hit it.

Ground Effects

BUTTER SIPPED FROM a bright, dark blue martini glass, trying to savor the bitter gin, working on a cosmopolitan mood. She had on her black-and-white op-art checkerboard pants and her pearlized white leather jacket, a new outfit that drew wonder from both her first-grade students and her Catholic school faculty colleagues. She considered herself striking. It was a pun, because she was depressed about her job and other aspects of life, and she was both privately and glaringly celebrating her protest. Almost every day she drove through downtown, coming from and going to teach, but she seldom parked and got out. What for? Today, though, after work, she had gone to the hotel to check out the last day of the Great Southern Culture Conference, to hear some exciting ideas. She had caught one session in a big carpeted room, and left after a windy-haired Asian man badly dramatized a paper that seemed to rail against existence.

A faintly fragrant man leaned in beside her and signaled the bartender. Butter glanced enough to notice mostly his sleeve—tropical wool navy with thin chalk stripes.

"Excuse me, Bud," the man said to Butter.

Lonnie Welcome smiled down at her. He looked sunned. She hadn't seen him in months, almost a year. He had stopped coming by Grim's and she had stopped phoning him. "No one's called me 'Bud' since I was four years old. I have been just that fortunate."

"Who called you Bud before me?"

"Some guy at a Yankees game. My parents took me."

He said, "Move it, Bud; you-se in my seat."

"I thought you were from Pittsburgh."

"Philadelphia. We were on vacation in New York."

"Oh. Nothing says city like Pittsburgh, though. I could have sworn that was your town."

"See. You should have stayed in love with me. You could've got straight on all that."

"Yeah. I could have watched your eyes turn green and your hair turn red. It's never been quite that short, has it?" He still smiled, but he lifted an eyebrow, as if suggesting her cosmetic choices were too vivid.

"Sure it has. I have it professionally barbered. You really missed out. Still, you recognized me."

"I thought you were Bud."

When the bartender came over, Lonnie ordered club soda. A small diamond glittered on his nose, which Butter pointed to. "That's daring."

"It hurts, too. I just got it." He made a face as though he was disgusted with himself, or with the world that would support his putting a diamond in his nose. "It reminds me of you, a hard precious thing that keeps my nose open."

"Hey, you left *me* hanging."

"You went back to Grim."

"I never *left* Grim."

"Well, then, good. We're both feeling mean. I'm in the right section."

Butter laughed a little bit. The bartender brought Lonnie's club soda. Tiny bubbles, backlit by the counter lights behind the bar, traveled up the glass and spritzed out of the top like bright little sparks. When Lonnie sipped the drink, the rim of the glass and his nose jewelry flared.

Around the bar, other conference-goers, just dislodged from concurrent sessions, occupied the round marble-top tables. Men sprawled slightly, with loosened ties, on comfortable-looking green leather sofas, but the women kept more elegant postures, their long fingers fondling wineglass stems, bracelets slipping along their wrists.

"What are you doing here, anyway?" she asked, biting an olive off the red plastic toothpick from her glass.

"A panel prop. They got me here as a kind of image consultant. Commercial images of the South, like that."

She gave a skeptical look.

"My company thought I should do it. We had some very scholarly types in the audience, though, I must say.

Women with dreadlocks and half-glasses, calling *them-selves* mammies. As commercial images go, now that's an oldie-goody. I thought it was dead."

"A mammy is a good thing, now. A good word. They're reappropriating the image, taking control of it, so it's not a negative."

"I know what they're doing. I just wonder who they're trying to convince."

"Well, I doubt if it matters too much, as Grim would say."

"Then there were these white folks who kept talking about black people as products. Something about 'body commodity' and 'cultural economics.' Space-age evil if you ask me."

"But that's down your alley, isn't it? *You* produce and sell the images."

"Yeah, yeah, well I don't confuse the image with the actual—which is what they were doing."

"Yeah, yeah, yeah."

A stool became free down the bar and Lonnie went to fetch it. He carried it in one hand, his coat unbuttoned and his tie swinging as he walked. The tie was a solid dark green, the knot tiny. A white handkerchief peaked from the pocket of his jacket. Lonnie looked good in a suit, the trouser fabric draping beautifully from his black, silver-buckled belt to the tops of his black suede shoes. It was a good suit.

"Is Grim here somewhere?" He bumped the stool onto the space of carpet she had made for him.

"Grim wouldn't come to anything like this. You know he has no ego."

"Oh, yeah. Well, me either."

"Right."

"But look at you, though. A whole new artificial hybrid. What must you think of yourself?"

"You don't like it?"

"I want to see your real eyes."

"These are my real eyes. Those other eyes were fake. You think I can't be black and change my hair and eyes? It's a new day, brother man. I'm with the sisters at your session. Beyond them. I'm a new stereotype, is what I am. I'm not a black woman trying to look white; I just look like one."

"And I'm attracted to the irony, I'm ashamed to say. What does that make me?"

"Negroid Typicalis."

Lonnie tilted up his glass and chewed an ice cube. He looked at her sideways. "But you're still my nigger, right?"

"Ha. Not hardly."

He smiled toward his sparkling glass, which he rotated on the bar with his fingertips. Butter felt a surging trace of tenderness for him, from that wild day when she was determined to seduce him, from those weeks when she was willing to be in love with him if such an alchemy of emotions could be achieved. He couldn't care enough for her to overcome Grim, or his superstitions about his drug use. While it seemed she *could* overcome Grim, and Lonnie's wobbly sobriety, she couldn't care enough to persist after his weird dismissal of her. And finally she had felt glad that he dropped away, and achieved a glum relief. Besides, it was almost effortless to be with Grim, sadly so. Still, she had missed Lonnie.

Butter turned from the bar as a lady wearing a long

green African-style dress and hat swept into the room, the rich-looking fabric dotted with soft-edged purple and gold squares. She seemed regal but she didn't look African. She stopped one of the cool, busy waitresses, the shapely Somalian-looking girl in the extraordinary high, cork-soled shoes. They conferred, and the waitress pointed a very long arm and finger toward the glass doors, and then let the arm flow slowly to the right. Butter nudged Lonnie, who swiveled for a view of the women. The lady smiled, nodded at the waitress, glanced around and left quickly.

"What?" Lonnie said.

"Must be some other function."

Lonnie shrugged, and swiveled back. "Are we a secret?"

"Huh?"

He pointed to himself and then to her.

"Oh." She sighed, and propped her cheek on her hand. "I don't know, Lonnie. You want to be a secret?"

"It's tempting."

"I didn't discuss it with Grim. He probably suspects. The thing about it is, he's old enough to be my daddy. My really young daddy, though. And anyway, he's a pretty wise dude. He figures that I'll get over the curiosity of youth, and either I'll stay with him or I'll move on. Except I'm twenty-seven, already. I mean, like I said, he doesn't seem to want much. Or he doesn't expect to keep anything he gets."

"I'm only old enough to be your brother. Your really old brother. I may not be so wise. But I hope it's clear that I always wanted you, and I wasn't too afraid of Grim.

I was reinventing myself at the time, and I hadn't gotten all my new fingers and toes yet. My new skin was too sensitive, too. I had to stay away until right about this minute."

"Well, of course." She regarded him seriously. "Your problems were pretty bad, I guess. That's the thing, see. I like Grim's contentment and I liked your other thing. Your disturbance—is that it?"

"Yeah, that's it." He put money on the bar, enough for her drink, too, which she couldn't finish after all. "Let me see your eyes."

"No."

"Come up to my room, then. I want to change clothes. I gotta twist this rock in my nose, and it's an unseemly sight in public."

"You have a room? Why? Are you from out of town, now?"

"Come on, Butter, pretend you kept up with me. Act like you know I moved to the country, that I have my own municipality, my own mayor and recycling program, that I'm a powerful and generous man."

"I don't know, Lonnie. I feel like pudding. Like ooze, now. I'll go to your room, sure. Just to spread out on the floor. Besides, my mother told me a lady never sits alone at a bar. I just remembered that. I'm not supposed to chew gum, either. She would keep me home from school when it rained. And I never went camping with Girl Scouts." She climbed off the stool and slipped on her loafers, which she had kicked under the brass foot rail. "So, are you a king or something."

"Of course."

At the elevators, a crowd of people waited to get on and a crowd of people flooded out. Butter and Lonnie let the people swirl around them, and finally boarded a car with a handsome, hand-holding, square-shaped couple, who reminded Butter of dolls—their formal clothes so crisp and their faces so benignly placid. The man wore a silk tuxedo and the woman an ivory beaded dress. They had matching olive complexions and lustrous straight black hair, as smooth and luxuriously somber as gourmet-market eggplant. The elevator went down, and when the door opened on the basement the doll-like couple didn't move.

"You're vegetarians," Lonnie said.

For a moment, Butter was shocked. She thought he had said "vegetables."

The couple looked at him with broadening smiles. He said, "I'm a vegetarian, too. Your skin is so beautiful. You must live only on fruit. I want to look as beautiful as you."

Butter, shocked again, said, "You do," and the couple and Lonnie muttered "Thank you." They rode up, sneaking peeks at one another, in awkward silence. It occurred to Butter that no one had complimented her, and she would have liked that, just to make their group a package.

Butter followed Lonnie along the rose-colored sixth-floor corridor, and watched him slip a key card into the door. His room was a small suite, basically taupe, with shiny drapes and a satiny striped sofa. Lonnie tossed the key card on the coffee table and went into the bedroom. "I'll be right back."

Butter opened the carved armoire to reveal the television and refrigerator. From the latter she took out a ginger ale and a jar of cashews. She read the price list taped to the door and shouted, "I'm costing you a fortune in here."

"O.K.," he shouted back, and Butter realized there was no need to shout.

After awhile, she shouted, "I'm sitting on your sofa. I'm going to call my mother."

He shouted back, "I'm putting my shoes back on."

He didn't come out right away. Butter took out her contacts, which had begun to feel like bark in her eyes. She floated them in pools of ocular solution and snapped them away in their case. She watched the sky pinken through the window across the room. It was the start of a pretty, early-autumn sunset. The mornings and evenings had been cool this week, and the season's change made her mildly anxious. She consciously forced herself to sit still and wait for Lonnie, to stop shaking her foot, to not get up and pace about. She didn't slip off her shoes or take off her jacket. She stopped chewing the delicious cashews. She only allowed herself to blink and breathe, and pretended to be as calm as the couple on the elevator. I'm a living doll, she told herself.

"Hey, Lonnie, I'm maturing out here. You'd better come see this. Quick."

When he finally reappeared, she was slouched on the sofa, her knees spread apart, her bare feet resting atop her shoes, her brown eyes staring at the lovely coral sky. "I'm not drunk and I'm not seductive. Don't look at me like that."

"Well, what are you, then?"

"Don't know. I was a spitfire once. On the move. Now I have this tension, see, between stop and go, stop and go. I keep having a dream about a dead boy."

"Oh." He sat down beside her. "Are my pants glowing?" They were brown brushed cotton, with a slight iridescence in the room's fading light.

"They do have a sheen. Now and then. And your shirt—is that fruit punch? The shirt inspires comment, too."

He held her hand, which was limp, palm up at her side. "I don't want you to be sad tonight. You look very pretty. We should get something to eat to cheer you up."

She turned to him and blinked her eyes rapidly. Stopped. Then blinked them fast again.

"Oh, yeah. I get it. It's really you, now."

She rested her head on his shoulder. "Grim's daddy is sick. He's gone to Florida to see him. That's why he's not here, another reason, anyway."

"Grim has a father?"

"Yeah." She laughed. The room was losing light. The dark surface of the coffee table had a peculiar dull luster, as if a layer of light had been scraped off with a dinner knife.

"So this dead boy I'm dreaming about. I visited him once. My parents took me to his house, way down the street from mine. He was about my age and in a wheelchair. We were six. And he didn't go to school, because he had soft bones, my mother said. Or fragile bones. They were easily broken. I was afraid of him because he was stick-man thin. And he had a silent expression, as though he could do without me watching him trying to smile for his mother. It was probably some kind of pain control. So then he died that same year and we went to the wake at the funeral home. I never asked why he died, but I wondered if he had tried to walk and his mere weight had caused his skeleton to collapse. Or if he had fallen out of bed and pulverized himself. So at the wake his mother told me that her powdered, bow-tied boy was just asleep. And that, you know, was worth imagining. Except *I* knew he wouldn't wake up. So anyway, now I'm dreaming about him all the time and it's bumming me."

"You didn't call your mother, did you?"

"Nope."

"You know who's a good mother, I think? Grim's sister, Rita. She raised him, and then she adopted all those girls. Nothing wrong with any of them."

"She should have been our mom, then. But her husband would have been our dad, and he would have named us for Chevrolets: Monte Carlo and Caprice."

"That would be all right." He got up and walked to the window. He was a silhouette against the sky's burgundy glow.

"Well, Rita's not perfect, anyway. I mean she's a genius of kindness but she hates her father. She won't even acknowledge he exists. Grim had to go down there by himself, even when the man's wife died some months ago. Not Grim's mother. Plus, she's on lithium, which I don't think explains it. I mean, he abandoned them and all after their mother died. So that's it, really."

"And there was that weird kidnapping a couple of years back. Or drunk driving. What was that about?"

"Hey, that was serious. I mean, you couldn't doubt her even if you didn't believe her. Which I did, anyway. A good person like her would have to be evil for that to be a lie. So she's a good mother. She has my vote even if she is a little scary."

"Isn't that her there?"

Butter sprang up and ran to the window. They looked down on the parking lot. Several women and men in fancy African dress strode across the lot toward the building. Some of the men wore tuxedos, a few in kinte-cloth hats. "Where is Rita?"

"There, by the purple." He gestured straight down, and Butter had to go on tiptoe to see.

A woman wrapped in yards of shiny cloth stood by a car with purple ground effects. "Wow." It was a silver Jag, and it cast an unearthly purple glow that tinted the exhaust from the tailpipe, absorbed the meager red and amber rays from its parking lights, and made itself seem to float. "It looks like a nuclear secret," Butter said.

A man came up behind the woman and put his arm around her waist. It was clearly not Mayes, Rita's husband. The man was white, or very light-skinned, in a plaid dinner jacket, and his face was pale purple in the radiance.

"That's not Rita. She wouldn't be in that car."

"Would you?" he asked, as if it was out of the question, as if he hadn't pierced his nose and she hadn't dyed her hair red. "It's made of plutonium."

"Oh, hell, yeah. Can't you see me in it? Just pull up and toot the horn. Then slide over. That's the Milky Way."

Swoon Time

LIKE ANYONE WHOSE work does not involve family, Mayes led a double life. In each he was able essentially to ignore the other, occasionally marveling at that ability.

One day he's driving a blue Chevy van in the cool green of Boone, NC, on his way with his hip-hopping daughters and his unlimited wife to a kids' soccer tournament. The next he's speeding through scorching Louisiana heat in an orange convertible Catalina with a woman who has met him at the airport; thank God the top is up.

The woman was a member of the Lyceum committee,

and she was driving him around until his hotel room was ready. She said raccoons ate the car's air-conditioning. Mayes was trying to come down from the plane trip, which was like riding in a buffeted beach ball. He could still recall the face of the young fat man who sat across the aisle. The man wore a red knit shirt and had thick black hair parted on the side. His face, flushed red with sweaty anxiety and hypertension, held the suffering of everyone on the plane. They all thought they were going to die.

The car skimmed along a narrow two-lane country road past barbed-wire fence and black cows. Mayes counted the seconds until they reached the cool oak shadows that bounced the Catalina back into the heat. Something in the ditches and fields kept buzzing. Crickets, bees, or cicadas. The driver wore her blond hair slicked back and sported black Wayfarers. She looked like a movie star. "You want to see our rotten culture." The car hugged a curve and Mayes had to look up at her. Out the window the sky was where the field and cows should have been.

"Where are we?" he asked, hearing his briefcase slide on the backseat and thump into the door. He went to school in this town. He had grandparents buried here. He and Rita had planned their futures from here.

"We're here. Good, he's home."

She jammed a dusty boot on the brake and turned onto a bumpy path. Suddenly they were enshaded, gratefully cooled, in something like a barn. A man looking like a pirate leaned against a pitchfork. He opened Mayes's door and ushered him out. The barn had a straw floor. This wasn't a barn exactly, but a big arbor—trees and vines over a latticework shell. Sun dapples dotted the place. The driver said, "Randal, this is our guest of honor."

"Welcome. Now what shall we call you? Guest? Mr. Honor? *Ours?*"

"Mayes. Got anything to drink?"

"You brought him to the right place, Cola. I have new recipes."

Cola, the driver, whose name Mayes had forgotten as soon as she had offered it at the airport, motioned to follow Randal. Randal now looked less a pirate. He did have an Errol Flynn mustache, but his long sideburns were royal blue; he wore a hoop earring in each ear and each eyebrow, and his bandanna cap was peach. He had on faded blue overalls and black hightop All-Stars.

Mayes followed Randal through a door hidden in shadow at the back of the arbor and entered a wood-floored room with log-cabin walls. Cola sat at an aluminum and Formica table, and Mayes joined her, while Randal got behind a shiny pine bar. He pulled pitchers and fruit from a bronze-toned refrigerator and started loading a couple of blenders.

As the blenders started to whir, a yellow long-faced dog in a ruffled red-and-white apron trotted from behind the bar. "That's Monkey," Cola said, and Monkey started to walk back and forth on her hind legs. When the whirring stopped, she propped her paws on the bar top and watched Randal pour the drinks.

On the wall just above Mayes's head was a framed black-and-white photograph of a man dressed in a tightly buttoned plaid overcoat and a puffy plastic cap with fur-lined earflaps. He stood hugging an ax in front of an open shed piled haphazardly to the top with split logs. Cola said, "That's me."

It looked nothing like Cola. It was a man who looked black, though pale-skinned; he looked retarded. His grin indicated an absurd pride and joy about all that cut wood.

"What do you mean?" Mayes asked.

Randal delivered the frothy drinks in turquoise metal glasses. "Yep, that's me."

Maybe the man's name was Me, Mayes thought. Maybe that's what they meant.

"Relax." He sat down, and Monkey walked on hind legs back behind the bar and dropped out of sight. "Monkey's the best dog ever. She has only three months to live. I want her to experience more in life than any other dog, within reason. She deserves that much."

"She's a special dog," Cola said, touching Randal's shoulder.

"I noticed it right away."

Randal looked cheerful again and raised his glass. "To good dogs and the good life."

The drink was bluish and sweet. Mayes couldn't decide whether or not it was alcoholic. He kept thinking it's swoon time; yet it had never been swoon time before. Monkey walked out into the open on all fours and lay down by Randal's chair. Cola complimented Mayes on his work and said she looked forward to hearing him speak.

"Cola is brilliant," Randal said. "She sculpts chocolate. You should see. You *will* see."

"There will be fashion models there," Cola said. "It should be quite a celebration."

Mayes closed his eyes and basked in the coolness of the

room, of the metal glass in his palm. The ceiling fan turned slowly overhead. He tried to remember the opening lines to his speech, but what came to mind was the beach. Large waves rolled in from the ocean. He stood on the back deck of a gray beach house watching surfers ride the curls. The surfers hunched over like gorillas. They hit the beach carrying automatic weapons and stormed the house. He knew he was in a cartoon, yet still he was frightened by the gorillas. Their eyes were red and water sprayed from their fur as they leapt out of windows with women from the house. The women screamed for help as they were taken out to sea, but one gorilla pinned him with a hand to his chest.

He awakened with his cheek on the table. He could see the other two turquoise tumblers, but Cola and Randal weren't in their seats. They stood at the bar with Monkey.

"How long was I out?"

Monkey barked once.

"Not long," Cola said. "There's something on your face."

He still felt numb and drowsy. He picked a leather coin from his cheek. It had the silhouette of what looked like a mosque etched into it, and the words "girls, girls."

"My calling card," Randal said. "For my next life."

"It's how we'll recognize him," Cola replied.

"Fine. But what about my room? Am I supposed to meet Dr. Loom?"

"Just be careful. I'm in love with Dr. Loom, and Randal is in love with me."

"Aren't you married?" Randal asked.

"Yes, of course." Mayes showed his hammered-gold band.

"Ecstatically?"

Mayes smiled at that. He sipped his sweetish drink, daring it to be dangerous, hoping it was not. "My wife is a pharmaceutically dampened clairvoyant, with eye-popping beauty. I'm scared to death of her. Her eyes, by the way, are like river pebbles. She's the one who's ecstatic."

Cola and Randal glanced at each other. "May we quote you?" Cola asked.

"I can't know if that's good news."

"It's true affection." Mayes looked at Cola. She had pushed her sunglasses on top of her head; her irises were blue as tropical fish.

"Well, I don't trust scientists," Randal said. "No offense. But you guys lack squeamishness. You're the dispassionate types that serial-kill."

"Not me," Mayes said. "I'm not dispassionate, just curious. No offense, indeed."

"Curious about what, after all?"

"Well, let me think. I *am* looking forward to your next life." He grinned evilly. He held up the leather coin.

Randal stroked Monkey's head. "Yeah, O.K. Moi, too. Anyway, I'll be at your party. Monkey, aussi, maybe. She's a party dog."

"Cool. Guess what. That old black magic's got me in a spin."

The hotel was new on the university campus. The lobby was light and drizzly, gentle sprinklers watering the pale green plants along the red-slate paths that bordered the carpeted lounges, the registration desk, the elevator alcove. The air was cool, though Mayes kept forgetting he was not in a greenhouse, sunlight streaming through the tall glass walls. It was in his room that he felt oriented. There was a bed among some tables and chairs. The telephone's red message light blinked.

Cola took off her white shirt and sat in a chair by an air vent. Her bra was white, which he could see through her shirt, anyway. She wore black jeans. She fanned her knees open and shut. Her shoulders and chest were freckled. He couldn't see that through the shirt.

"Are you interested in this kind of thing?"

"Sure." Mayes looked out the sliding door to the balcony, which was an outside corridor protected by a railing, extending the breadth of the U-shaped building. He could see all the floors across the small grassy courtyard. His sense of privacy in the small dim room was challenged by the comprehensive view. Workmen on the fourth floor were hoisting furniture over the railing and dropping it into large green Dumpsters below.

"I've never been in a hotel like this one."

"It's shedding its skin."

"I like that sound when the furniture hits. Bahoom. Somebody should record that."

"Oh, I got it already. It's the latest craze, the sound of deconstruction."

"There's newer stuff, isn't there? Or is that the point —instant nostalgia? Is this whole town smart?"

"I wish."

"Why are they doing that?" He indicated the workmen.

"Economics, probably. Everything is economics."

Mayes considered that response. She folded her arms and jiggled her foot.

"Sex, too. Everything is also sex," she said. "But that's just a theory."

She gnawed some on her bottom lip. Mayes stared at her. He wondered if she hadn't really been in the movies. "Well, if you really listen to it, I guess it's sexy. Sub-disturbing. Boom."

"That's right."

He hung his clothes in the closet and began to put things in the dresser—socks, shirts, shaving tools. "This is just a conversation. That's all. Academic. Besides, when I'm around young women in their underwear my stomach starts to droop and hang over my belt. My chest turns to flab. It's a new thing but it happens."

"What about the old thing?"

"That happens, too. Thankfully."

She lifted her shirt from the bed and put it on.

"You're not moving in?"

"Nope. It was a trick. I just wanted to get cool. I think skin should be cool. I'm cool now. But, just so you know, my thighs are freckled, too."

He zipped his suitcase and stowed it in the closet. Across the way the workmen dropped bureaus, drawers, bed frames, and headboards into the truck bed. Mayes slid open the door. Cola turned on the television to a talk show and stretched out on the bed. A headboard sliced through the air from the balcony above Mayes's room. "Fire in the hole," a workman yelled. "Three pointer," someone else shouted. A coffee table tumbled down. "Incoming," said a voice. An armoire streaked by. Boom! He closed the door and muffled the noise. The truck beds below were crammed with broken furniture.

When the talk show went off, Cola picked up the phone and dialed for Mayes's messages.

"Dr. Loom's meeting you for dinner, or you can skip that and rest awhile before the lecture."

"Rest," Mayes said. "Why don't you get going? See the sights. Find me something sweet to eat, some of those soft red, sugar-coated strings my daughters like."

"Whatever."

"Thank you."

"How about some gobs of great yummy crap? I know where a lot of that is."

"Perfect."

"There's a message from your wife, too. She says to call her, that something's wrong, but not urgent."

After Cola left, Mayes lay stripped to his shorts, air conditioner off, wide door open. For now, the blue-sheeted bed was a raft and Louisiana's warm wet air was a pool. The light was watery through the blue window sheers, a breeze wafting shadows over the room. The workmen were going home for the day.

He wanted to go over his speech. This was the university that granted him his degree, where he and Rita totaled the number of kids they'd try to have, after moving here from North Carolina, after they were married, after Grim was sent away to boarding school, after Rita got control of and was treated for her mania. He had studied here partly because this was where his grandparents were born and where they died, partly because of the fellowship he was offered. His parents had left here—escaped is how they had described it—before he was born. He had no idea who his great-grandparents were, but they must have been here once. He had wanted to give Rita some family and these were the deepest roots he could find. She did need some grounding, he thought, as liable as she was to zoom out of reach. Besides Grim, her only close family had been an aunt, now dead. When he answered her phone message, she repeated that something was wrong. But she didn't know what it was. He took it as a warning. Tonight he wanted to do well, as he had in school. This was as far back as he could go.

Cola picked him up at 6:30 and walked with him to the auditorium. She was now in a black-and-white silk sari, and she handed over the gummy candy. Shards of splintered wood and popped-loose screws littered the grass and the walkway through the courtyard. When they got free of the hotel and cut through the park, Mayes was surprised to see homeless people bedded down for the night. The sun had not even set. They lay covered on pallets under moss-draped oaks.

A balding, wire-haired man attracted Mayes's attention. He sat with a thin woman on a park bench. They didn't appear homeless, the man in polished wing-tip shoes and the woman in red lipstick. The man was irate. He told his companion the hotel furniture could be given to the homeless instead of shamelessly wasted by some bureaucracy. Who's responsible, he wanted to know.

What would the homeless do with it? Mayes wondered as he passed. He imagined wall-less rooms of arranged

furniture in the park. Made-up beds. Dark lamps with
limp unplugged cords. Sofas on the carpet of anthills and
grass. Rough-bearded men pulling pajamas out of dressers
at night and hunched over coffee at square tables in
the morning, fog rising in the dawn. He wondered if he
could slip that vision into his speech tonight. He laughed
to himself. The speech was about aerospace cryogenic
technology.

At the auditorium Dr. Loom introduced him as a "native son," and Mayes wished he hadn't. But the idea
seemed to please the sparse audience of grad students and
faculty. Dr. Loom was a tall elegant-looking man with
silky silver hair. He called Mayes "one of our own," and
a "local boy who made good," "the pride of our program,"
a "prodigal son" and a "gifted researcher."

Mayes took the podium to loud applause, and felt
shamefully fake. He only went to school here, and he only
did his job. There was nothing gifted, native, or boy about
him, he thought. Still, he gave his speech, but by the end
he was so deflated by the notion that nobody knew him
as he knew himself that he recklessly diverged onto the
homeless in the park. Trying to tie it to the theme of
measuring the temperatures of space. He wondered aloud
about people's comfort with limitless space. He said that,
given the chance, the people in the park would surround
themselves with the hotel's discarded furniture, which had
been exploding around him since he checked in. They
would set up roomlike boundaries as a hedge against the
wide-open.

He stood in a spotlight, the rest of the auditorium dark.
He could see down to the front row where Dr. Loom sat

beside Cola. Cola smiled at him, her necklace of clear glass reflecting white light bounced from the university seal on the podium. Paradoxically, he said, no matter how cold the limitless reaches, people are like air, always expecting to encounter more space. That, he said, is both the practical and the philosophical value of cryogenic technology.

The applause was polite, except for strong rhythmic clapping on the left side of the room. Mayes made out the weak gleam of Randal's silver rings bobbing with his nodding face.

Cola drove him to Dr. Loom's white-columned Georgian house near the campus. On a long dining-room table, slices of meats, cheeses, and breads were nestled on trays among bowls of pickles, olives, and cherries. Plates of pâtés, trays of small, shaped chocolates, and a large bowl of chicken wings covered one end of the table, along with a heavy tureen of seafood gumbo. In the center was a silver tray of peaches and grapes. The place was plush with thick rugs and green and burgundy velvet couches and chairs. There were even tasseled lamps, and dense paintings in gilded frames. Everything was soft and heavy and cool, the air-conditioned temperature very low.

People began filling the house, many who could not have been at the lecture. Cola lit short sticks of sweet, black incense, and placed them in small ceramic burners in various corners of the rooms. Dr. Loom joined Mayes by the fireplace and said he wasn't sure whether or not he liked Mayes's talk, until the end. "You got psychedelic there."

He looked away from Mayes as he spoke, as if he was

a spy pretending not to speak. Mayes couldn't remember ever standing with him in conversation. His nose, at that angle, seemed as sharp as a knife blade. His suit was beautiful blue silk and his blue silk tie subtly textured. Mayes looked away, too, and because he pretended that he was also a spy, it seemed easy to walk away.

Mayes wandered into another, less-populated room. One of the white-cloth-covered tables that functioned as bars was staffed by a stunning, red-lipped bartender. He wondered if she was one of the fashion models. Before Mayes could speak to her, Dr. Loom was beside him again.

"I meant no offense. I'm only loosely affiliated with the university now. Emeritus, you know. But I asked for the privilege of introducing you, coming from the program I care for."

They faced the bartender instead of each other. Dr. Loom touched his long finger to a bottle of bourbon on the table, and the bartender poured into a shallow plastic cup of ice. Then he pointed to a pitcher of water.

"You know, my family freed the slaves." It was difficult to know who he was talking to. The bartender frowned and straightened her bottles.

"Please, then," Mayes said, "thank them for me." He eyed Dr. Loom peripherally.

Dr. Loom's thin white eyebrows performed some graceful arcs, like wry curls of incense smoke.

"But you know, I can't say that was a good thing. It was 1863, just before the Emancipation Proclamation. I must have told you this years ago. Anyway, my maternal great-great-granddaddy told his slaves to leave."

The bartender stopped her bother with the bottles. She crossed her arms and looked at Dr. Loom.

"Now can you imagine?" he continued. "You see, insanity runs in my family. Where were they going to go? They walked with their bundles out to the road and saw there was nothing out there, no place for them and no way to get there. You could say I come from cruel stock, or you could praise my magnanimous heritage. But I'm reminded of the time we had an African poet a couple of years ago, and there was a group of high-school students in the audience. He talked about the part of the continent he was from, and a young man stood and asked, 'How far a drive is that?' It is that kind of ignorance our slaves must have known."

The bartender looked at both Mayes and Dr. Loom before whirling around and busying herself with boxes of wine against a wall.

"Not unlike our heroic astronauts, say?" said Dr. Loom. "Whose travels you prepare for?"

Presenting her crisp, starched back, the bartender said, "Sir, those people your family enslaved and freed. What happened to them?"

"Why, I suspect that, like my ancestors, they perished."

Mayes regretted the loss of the bartender. As he left the room, Dr. Loom was holding out his glass toward her back, as if wanting his drink topped off. His silver cuff link sparkled.

In the kitchen Mayes was approached by another beautiful young woman, a student reporter for the campus newspaper. She had a whisk of raspberry-pink hair that ended neatly at the base of her skull, where the under-fuzz was dark. She wore tiny black shorts and horizontally striped, thigh-high stockings. Her white, wiry sweater bared her midriff. All her clothes seemed shrunken, exposing skin in unexpected places, yet she seemed to be wearing too much. Her purple fingernails were so long, they curved. She held a small recorder up to his face and asked if she might interview him now.

"Anyway, what did you mean tonight by that last part? The stuff about being air?"

"Just what I said. It was a metaphor."

"So," she said into the recorder, "it made sense?" She held the recorder back to his face. "You were searching, it sounded like."

"It made sense to me."

"Really?" They stared at each other awhile. She turned off the recorder, and then switched it back on. She looked disappointed, even through her kabuki-thick makeup. Her eyes grew wetter, as if about to cry. "But what's that got to *do* with anything?"

Mayes sighed with sympathy and annoyance. He started to explain, to try, but she switched off the recorder. The kitchen was crowded. An Arab-looking woman stepped in front of him wearing gossamerlike clothes, gold embroidery at her wrists and hems. She passed on the arm of a big-headed little boy. Cola entered carrying an empty silver tray. She smiled at him. Suddenly, Monkey lunged through the back screen door in a red ruffled dress and Randal tumbled in after her. She barked rapidly and skittered wildly on the white tile floor, unable to get footing. She veered to Cola, who tried to shield an old man in a tuxedo by pinning him against the refrigerator with her back. Then Monkey skidded toward Mayes, and the reporter shrieked, hopping away. She propped her paws on Mayes's chest, her eyes, tongue and tail all rolling in seemingly opposite directions.

Mayes clutched her behind the elbows to steady her and himself, trying to stop her back feet from dancing, and wound up two-stepping. People from other rooms crowded in to look and laugh. Dr. Loom squeezed through, his bony features creased in agitation. "Is that a dog in my kitchen? Is that your prissy dog?" he said, confronting Randal.

"Yes, sir," Randal replied. He grabbed Monkey around the waist and led her back outside, the dog on two feet and prancing, chin raised high and wrists bent. Dr. Loom followed them, leaving a tense impression of white, red and blue—and shiny black shoes.

Mayes went over to Cola, who was now smoothing the old man's satin tuxedo lapel. He took the silver tray from her other hand and set it on the counter. "Take me to my room." He tried to smile. She seemed reluctant to stop stroking the man's coat. Mayes smoothed the other lapel, which was cool, soft and glossy. The man had brown blotches on his cheeks the various sizes of tiddlywinks. He was as compliant as a corpse, his eyes wet with seeming gratitude.

In Cola's car, she, too, seemed relieved to be out of the house. She put the top down on the Catalina. The moon, which had lost some of its fullness, was clear, the grayish craters visible in the glow.

"Do people still go there?"

"I only feel a little bit sad," Mayes said. As they drove away, he noticed Randal dancing with Monkey between two parked cars on the street. In the narrow space they looked almost graceful.

Cola's sari fluttered in the wind. They didn't speak for a while. They sped along a wet, unfamiliar avenue, water streaming down in rivulets and waves. After a curve they saw the water gushing from a silver hydrant that shone under a streetlight. When they passed it, they seemed to burst through a pool of silver water and light, the hydrant pushing water in the car at the sound of Cola's scream, the swish of tires, and with the quick cold drench of Mayes's right side.

Cola stopped the car. "Was that sudden?"

The silk stuck to her right breast, until she noticed Mayes's gaze and plucked the wet fabric from her skin. "I should have worn a brassiere, I guess."

"It had the effect of sudden."

"It was irresistible."

From the moment she pulled the silk from her breast, he had the feeling of déjà vu, but soon he couldn't sense beyond the present, which was bluish-green dashboard lights glimmering in the wet glass discs of her necklace; a gust of wind waving the trees on the side of the road; the wipers swiping the windshield once; a long circus-lighted truck passing on the overpass in front of them.

"I think maybe I was born here."

Cola looked around, as if searching for the exact spot. "Right this moment?"

"In this town, silly child."

"Oh. You scared me. I thought you had gained control

of the freaky. And ease up with the 'silly child' thing. You ought to know better."

"Sorry." He blotted his face with a handkerchief from his jacket pocket and then offered it to her.

"So why hadn't you said something before? Here I was thinking you were a guest. Are you mixed up in something?"

"I can't tell you."

"You think you're haunting the place? You've come back as a ghost?"

"I'm being rude. Ignoring the town."

Cola tossed the handkerchief back to him and pulled away from the curb. When they had gone under the bridge, she said, "Who knew you had such conceit?"

"Yeah, I know. I was fine, though, until Dr. Loom turned out to be Abe Lincoln's grandson."

"Really? He's a sleek old blue guy, isn't he?"

"He's familiar."

"So, were you born here or not?"

"My grandparents were. My parents were. I was conceived here at least."

"Then you *are* a homeboy."

"No, thanks. My parents couldn't stand the place. They got the hell out of Dodge."

"The way I see it, this whole world is Dodge. Get it?"

"I get it all the time."

She kept her gaze toward the road. Traffic was thin. They made a few turns and approached the campus hotel. "Well, tomorrow, you'll be flying away again. So shouldn't I take you somewhere? Your folks' old neighborhood?"

"It's not there."

She steered the car into the university hotel parking lot and stopped at the gate to the courtyard. She turned off the headlights but kept the motor running. Lamps on hook-shaped poles shone down on them. One of the big green Dumpsters crowded the gate.

"Listen, I really wanted this to be pleasant for you. Instead, you get falling furniture, harassed by Dr. Loom, and kissed by Randal's dog. But you knew there was nothing I could do about your history here."

"I appreciate the models, though. If you ever visit me at my place, bring them, too."

"Your wife, remember?"

"Of course. And my children. Don't forget them."

"You know, I'm very lovely, myself."

He kissed Cola on the cheek. Her skin was marshmallow soft. "The falling furniture, I haven't minded that at all."

Out of the car he squeezed past the Dumpster. The Dumpster was filled to overflowing with dropped furniture, edges jutting out like chiseled stone. Popped-loose brass hinges glittered dully in the grass. They looked like perfectly good hinges, and he bent to pick up a few. When he stood up and looked back, Cola was driving away. Across the street the park was dark, with dim lumps of homeless people sleeping on the ground. Thin, lit clouds moved across the sky near the moon.

The next morning a light rain was falling. From his window Mayes watched a TV crew filming the furniture movers. Evidently, someone had had enough, and now there would be a local scandal. Someone could be shamed.

Someone else could use the furniture after all. Still, the workers showed off. "Fast ball," one of them yelled, as a square table flipped down from the balcony above him.

When Mayes left the hotel, the rain was heavy, the movers had stopped, and the TV crew was gone. This time Cola had parked the car at the hotel's main entrance, and Mayes entered from under the hotel's sheltering awning. From there he didn't see the homeless anywhere. The street glistened dark gray, and in the park puddles teemed in front of the gleaming-wet benches. The park lights and streetlights were still on, faint in the gray light of the day. The park's large, black, bowl-like fountain spouted water high into the air.

Cola circled out of the hotel driveway. She didn't say anything, as if the rain had drowned her resolve to entertain him. He was already yesterday's guest, he figured, had already worn out his welcome. Just the same, she smiled, and so did he, and he decided that they were sharing a sadness. Rain drummed loudly atop the car's cloth roof.

They stopped at a red light, and Mayes discovered the homeless huddled outside the school's planetarium that bordered the park. They huddled out of the rain under the eaves and in the alcove. Some stood, and others crouched or lay curled, all under blankets.

A car horn sounded behind them, but the traffic light was still red. A black limousine had pulled up to the curb. A man wearing a belted black trench coat and a dark homburg got out. A few of the people crept down the planetarium steps and got in the car, and the man drove them away. He seemed familiar to Mayes. It wasn't Dr. Loom but it was someone tall, thin and pale. Mayes couldn't determine if he had seen the man before or if the man simply resembled somebody else he knew.

Suddenly, the rain fell with such volume that Mayes could barely see the people still huddled in the alcove. "Who was that?" he asked Cola, but she shrugged. He had heard stories in which the homeless were lured and harmed. But probably the man was kind, with a limo full of sandwiches. He probably wished he could help everyone and would be back to pick up the others, to feed them and to get them dry. Maybe he had a house staffed with nurses, doctors and counselors trained to heal their possible wounds.

The red light wouldn't change. The red multiplied in the raindrops on the windshield, before the wipers smeared them. When the windows began to fog, Cola lowered hers a little. Mayes lowered his, too. The rain sounded like a loud, strident shush.

Cola reached for a bag in the backseat and handed it to him. "I was going to give you this at the airport. But this light is stuck, I guess. We may never get there."

He lifted out a heavy object wrapped in waxed paper, one of Cola's chocolate works. It was a breast, cupcake-size, toffee-colored, with a pink aureole and nipple. It had brown chocolate freckles sprinkled on it.

"Take me with you. But keep me cool. I melt."

Mayes laughed, grateful to Cola for distracting him, glad he hadn't spent his time in a cemetery looking for his grandparents' graves. He had found them once, when he was a student, but before he graduated he forgot where they were. Besides, he thought, with a shock of small fear, by tonight he would have flown at thirty thousand feet home to his family, landing where everything else he could possibly forget would come rushing up to meet him.

Mayes's first day back was the strangest. His twin lives seemed joined at the neck. Because he wanted to be there before the staff policy meeting to discuss the new rules being proposed for the labs, he left home early. The day was humid and drizzly. Randal's leather coin and Cola's candy breast were in his briefcase. He stopped short on the walkway when he saw a gorilla kneeling in the pink impatiens beside the building's steps. When it slowly moved, it was a black-skinned man in a gray hooded parka pulling weeds from the flower bed. The morning sky was like a spread of gray felt. He took the steps two at a time, and felt dizzy as he stared at the revolving door. He caught the reflection of his own dark face in the turning glass panels. He stepped forward, thinking everybody had better watch out, and swoosh—he was sucked into the gray, gleaming lobby.

The meeting was in progress. Mayes nodded silently at the faces around the room while the efficiency consultant explained orange and yellow columns on a bar graph. After awhile Mayes had no clue about the topic. He was still amused about the distant weirdness of his weekend. Many of his colleagues, he noticed, turned red. What was the consultant talking about? Thunder rolled in the walls. The recording secretary was crimson, her ears and hands by Gauguin. The old guy, of leather books and bird-dog suspenders, was a glowing pipe bowl. The room was full of tomatoes, and of lampshades covered with red satin shawls. The new lady, her cheeks like fuzzy peaches, crossed her legs in killer, cherry patent-leather boots, ready for the rain.

A woman came in and broke up the meeting. Thunder rolled into the room. Twisters were out there, she said. Take cover. The recording secretary burst into tears. Mayes's cellular phone trilled faintly in his briefcase. The consultant's hair seemed to flame, and Camaro told Mayes that her grandfather was dead. "You don't *have* a grand-father."

"I *know*. They're *all* dead." He imagined her rolling her teenage eyes.

Then he remembered Rita's father, a man he had never met. They had discovered him a year ago only to reignore him. Rita's brother had been in touch with him, but Rita was unforgiving.

"Are you at school?"

"No, Dad. Mom's packing to go to Florida. She wants you to pick up the youngsters."

"What's the weather where you are?"

"Stormy. Does lightning enter cellular trails?"

"What?"

"Let's hang up, O.K.?"

He was in his golden car, the windows tight, and the sky ocean-green. A layer of yellow behind that. Power lines along the interstate looped in the wind. The rain was a loud, cloudy wet mirror and Mayes was afraid of the trees.

He slipped off the interstate, barely seeing, and went toward the whirling trees. He imagined his daughters looking out the school windows at the yellow-green sky, the sheets of thick, fogged mirror falling. Daddy's coming, he signaled, thinking of Rita, his briefcase a mess of melted breast, her anonymous father more removed than ever.

Such sensitive skin, he thought of his colleagues. How did they ever know? He thought of Cola, her underwater eyes. He crashed through the flooded, teeming exit ramp, silver balls popping from the sky.

Massive Injuries

NOTHING IS EVER RIGHT. That was Butter's feeling after Grim's father died, and later after Grim nearly killed himself crashing his motorcycle into a telephone pole during the drive to Florida for the funeral. I told you so, damn it, Butter thought. Old fool on a motorcycle.

Grim experienced a feeling similar to hers when he hit the oil slick and skidded.

Two weeks later, one week after Thanksgiving, in his hospital bed, he was again aware of the disappointment. Though he was unconscious—hooked up to machines—

and didn't know where he was, didn't know his right cheek was shattered, his ribs crushed, his lung punctured, his arms and legs broken, his left foot reattached at the heel, his head swollen twice its size, his retinas detached, his scalp sewn down, his heart bruised, didn't know a hole was drilled in his fractured skull to accommodate the trauma-big brain, didn't know that screws were twisted into his temples to attach the halolike brace for his broken neck, naked under the sheets, under the casts, under the cotton, under the morphine, he thought of himself as the dog he'd once seen in somebody's flea-infested house. The dog's head had been fitted with an inverted lampshade to prevent it from biting its wounds. That dog— mottled and black, slow and fat—looked stupid and humiliated, and it kept walking through Grim's dream. It had Grim's face, which cringed inside the lampshade.

Butter stood with Lonnie at the foot of Grim's bed. She had been waiting for one of the doctors to arrive on rounds to predict something halfway positive. Two days before, Grim had been upgraded from critical to stable. (How? Butter wondered, looking at him.) Rita and Mayes had already flown back to Durham to look after their children, get them back to school, and arrange for Grim to be moved to a hospital nearer home. They had been eerily efficient, Rita having tamped down her anger at her dead father so tight she could handle Grim's misfortune with almost chilling, undistracted stoicism. No tears around Rita. Lonnie had shown up the day they left.

Lonnie thought Grim looked stable, all right. He

looked dead. Butter said she'd been waiting all morning
for the doctor. She wanted the doctor to guess when he'd
come back to consciousness. She wanted to know how he
would live.

Lonnie picked up the chart clipped to the bed and read
the parts that he understood. Grim's temperature was normal, so there was no infection. His blood pressure seemed
O.K. Lonnie could see when he'd been given medication.
He saw how much Grim voided. But he laughed when
he read Grim's name. Grim's name was Graham. It was
funny that Lonnie had never known. Maybe he had
known. It rang a bell.

"Did you know this?" he asked Butter, and pointed to
the name.

"Yeah. You didn't? Grim is Graham. It's how folks pro-
nounce it. It's not that funny."

But Lonnie kept laughing. That Graham was Grim's
name changed things a bit. He put the chart down and
laughed. He picked up the chart and read the name
again.

Butter took the chart away. "Act like you have some
sense. Suppose somebody comes in here."

"Yo," Lonnie said to Grim. "It's me, Lonnie. Me and
Butter. How are you feeling, Mr. Grim-Graham?"

The bed was tilted so that Grim was in a slight roll
position. Lonnie moved closer to his damaged head.

"Lonnie, please." Butter sighed. She touched one of the
swollen fingers that protruded from Grim's cast. "Do you
think he can hear you?"

"I hope so. You've been here every day, haven't you?
What do you think he can hear?"

"I've been trying to talk to him. Rita wants me to keep reading to him. I don't even know if that's Grim anymore."

"Well, you'd better not let him hear you say *that*. Might confuse him. Besides, he's not Grim anymore." He laughed a little more.

Lonnie sat in the chair beside the bed and watched Grim's chest move. The bedsheet covered Grim to his waist. He was strapped down. His torso was packed inside a thick pad of cotton, covered with a gray plastic shell. It looked itchy. "You are one lucky hombre."

Butter was crying, hugging herself, staring at the tilted, distorted Grim. Her long sheer skirt, mostly pale gold, swayed over her sandals as she rocked herself. She wore a white cotton sweater but was still cold in the chill of the room.

"Come here." Lonnie reached for her hand, and she sat awkwardly, half on the chair's green vinyl seat and half on Lonnie's lap. Lonnie scooted over so she could squeeze beside him, her hip pinching some of the cloth of his jeans. "Look how his left eye doesn't close all the way," he said. Butter wept.

Grim, the downcast dog, ambled out the screen door onto the back porch where cats lounged and glowered. There was a hole in the dirt under the porch, and Grim had to back himself down into it because of the lampshade. He settled awkwardly but comfortably into the cool dirt. His neck felt tight. He dozed. He was dreaming a dog's dream, which put him four-legged and dirty in a convenience store late at night, wearing the lampshade, and watching two wild-haired girls at the coffee station. One had hair as stiff and brown as pine straw, and drawn, black eyebrows. The other was platinum blond with a fur of fine hair on her face. She looked like a cat. The hair on her head was short and spiky, as if licked wet. When she turned with a plastic foam cup to face him, Grim said, "Hi." She didn't say anything. She wore beige Lycra pants and a black crocheted vest. She turned to the other girl, who wore a short denim skirt and purple high heels, and who had huge, shapely, showgirl legs.

"I wish we had some honey," she said.

Grim thought he should get some for her. He thought it was his obligation. He thought he was her dog, or somebody's dog, and he should be good about it.

"You got any honey?" she asked Grim.

The man who worked in the store said he had some. He came up beside Grim, but Grim could see only his shoes because of the lampshade. They were black rubber lace-ups. The cuffs of his blue pants pooled down onto them. While the man explained that the honey was in his car, Grim backed up because he did not like the clicking sound of his toenails on the tile. The man was gray-haired and thin with loose orange skin. His black belt was rubber like his shoes.

"I'll be right back," the man said.

When he left, the blond girl said, "We need a lemon instead of coffee."

"We're in the wrong place."

Grim wanted to leave, but he didn't want the girls to hear his toenails. He could hear something calling him. He looked around at the smooth, gray inside of the lampshade, and lay back down in the cool dirt under the house.

Butter sat in the chair beside the bed while Lonnie paced about the room. "Come out of there," she whispered to Grim.

A nurse's aide swept in, a sleepy-looking woman in pink pants. "How's our Graham today?"

"Jesus," Butter said. "How does he look?"

"Well, like there's room for improvement. But that's why we're here; isn't that right, Graham?" She measured Grim's temperature and pulse. She checked the I.V. and the urine bag. She adjusted the plastic tubes in his mouth and nose.

"Shouldn't a doctor be here by now?" Lonnie asked. "We only have his chart to consult."

"Soon. Everybody's running a bit behind. You might as well get some lunch. By the way, if you guys don't clip his nails, I will. Then he'll be mine all mine."

Lonnie looked to Butter. She had her shoulders drawn up, hugging herself.

"Go for it," he said to the aide. He took Butter into the hall.

"What's the matter?"

"I don't know. I'm sick."

Back in the room, in his dream, Grim was stuck in a jar of amber honey. He felt thick and clogged. It's better than hell, he thought.

Butter and Lonnie got their lunch and sat at a large round table. The cafeteria wasn't crowded. Butter recognized one of Grim's nurses and one of the nurses' aides sitting together across the room. She did a double take at the man sitting behind the nurses. For a moment she wasn't sure where she was. Belly Man was bent over a plate of spaghetti, and Tampa was not a place where she would see that. But it was Belly Man, all right. She pointed him out to Lonnie.

"Damn. He said he might come down. He wanted me to ride with him, but I got out of it. I sort of hoped that would mean he'd stay home."

"Well, he's here. He *is* Grim's friend."

"What am I?"

"My friend, as well."

"You will notice he's spending this quality time with food."

Butter headed over to Belly Man with her tray, and Lonnie followed. She said hello to the nurse and the aide. Belly Man regarded her solemnly. He swallowed what he had in his mouth. "How is he?"

Butter kissed his cheek and sat down across from him. "Stable, they say."

"Yeah, Rita told me that."

"No change, then," Lonnie said. "When did you get here?"

"Hey, you left me, man."

"I couldn't wait. I flew down a couple days ago."

Belly twirled a fork full of noodles. "I've been checking out the place. Can I see him?"

"Sure," Butter said. "You won't like it, though."

He grimaced, shook his head. "I hate hospitals, any-way." He put the roll of spaghetti in his mouth. Butter cut her liver and onions into bite-size squares. Lonnie didn't touch his hamburger.

"Grim's a tough man," Lonnie said. "A person should not have survived what he did. He'll probably pull through all the way."

"You know," Belly said, 'the last time I saw Grim was just before he came down here. We were over at Sonny's Gold Teeth. I was fooling with Sonny, and Grim was hooking up a car abandoned there about three days. That's when he told me his daddy was dead, and that he was getting ready to bike down here to free his head. That's what he said, 'free my head.' "

Butter nodded gently, and then gestured for the women's attention at the next table. "Excuse me." They stopped their conversation. "You've been taking care of our friend Mr. Power, in room 403."

"Yes, of course," said one. She was small and young, and had wispy blond curls for bangs, her hair pulled back and held with a large white plastic clip.

"We can't find his doctors," Butter said. "I have missed them every day. I just want to know what to expect."

They turned to each other for a second. Then the heavy one, the aide, said, "We're taking good care of him."

"That's not what she means." Belly Man was smiling. That was a good sign, Lonnie thought. "She wants to know about *him*."

Butter introduced herself as Phyllis, though she had at least greeted each woman before today. She gave the names of Belly and Lonnie, who pushed their chairs back to face the women. Lois and the aide, Della introduced themselves. Della's hair was buoyant and brown, a puffed

Prince Valiant shape around her plump, scrubbed face. Lois had sparkling blue eyes, with blue pencil rimming them and blue mascara on her lashes. The blue made her seem illusory, yet extra vivid, like color TV.

"What kind of recovery might he have? I mean, I know you don't know him. I wish you knew him as he really is."

"They are massive injuries, obviously," Lois said. "But he's coming along."

"Yep," Della said. "We've seen it before. You all need to keep doing what you're doing. Visiting. Talking to him. The stimulation is what he needs. Really."

Lois added. "The doctors can tell you a lot more."

"Thank you," Lonnie said.

"Do you play the lottery?" Belly Man asked.

"I beg your pardon?" Lois asked.

"Belly, really," Butter said.

"The Lotto," Belly Man repeated. "You guys have some huge jackpots."

Butter rubbed her temple and glanced from beneath her hand at Lonnie. Lonnie closed his eyes for a long moment, demonstrating tolerance. Lois, who had finished eating, piled her napkin and cutlery on her plate. With her finger, she brushed the corners of her mouth. "There are two ways to lose at the lottery. Not to play, and to play."

"Ha, that's a good one." Belly laughed.

Della said, "Well, I never hit the big one, but I won enough to get new living-room furniture last year. You sure can't win if you don't play."

"I heard that," Belly Man replied.

Lois stood and gathered up her tray. Her head down,

she said softly, "People have such opaque expressions of need."

They all stared at her.

"Whatever," Della said.

"Speak for yourself." Belly Man chuckled. "Anyway, what I'm wondering is, can you really win in this state? Specifically, can a black man win? Do you have to be in the right zip code or what? Naw, forget the whole state for a minute. Can my friend survive in this hospital, for instance? Back home, when I was like a teenager, my principal had hiccups for two months, and when he finally went to the hospital he died there within a week. You see my point? And some other black men, prominent peoples—a lawyer and a preacher, I know for sure—went in and died around the same time. People got to guessing they were feeding black folks arsenic in there."

"I remember that," Lonnie said. "It was kind of a joke, wasn't it?"

"Well, it wasn't a real funny one."

"Are you accusing us of criminality? Of being murderers?" Lois said. "You can't come in here talking like that."

"I can come in here and look after my friend, lady."

Butter said, "I don't know what you are all talking about. What about Grim—Mr. Power?"

"It depends." Della frowned and stood up with Lois. "You got to expect the best." She looked skeptically at all of them. "Paranoia won't help, believe me."

"There's nothing lacking in his treatment," Lois said, flushed. "But, you understand, as the doctors have surely said, his life might be very different."

"How?" Butter said, flicking her fingers wide.

Lois and Della looked at her sympathetically. "You'll need to speak with the doctors," Lois said. They left.

Butter struggled to let her frustration settle. She ate a piece of the liver. Then she asked, "Are you guys serious? You really believe those people were killed in the hospital?"

"You damn straight, I'm serious," Belly Man said.

"Nothing like that can happen now," Lonnie added. "Grim is quite safe, in that respect."

"Yeah, I'm on it," Belly Man stated.

Sometimes Grim wondered how the lampshade got there, but most of the time it was out of his mind. Besides, he kept reminding himself, he was a dog. He did meet another dog, named Johnny, and that dog didn't seem to care about Grim's lampshade. He had a thing against cats, to which, unashamedly, he was also attracted. Johnny was charcoal gray, with clear brown eyes—a handsome dog. He jumped out of a Jeep parked at a post office that Grim was waddling by.

He asked if Grim had seen a couple of "feline lambs." Their description matched the women at the convenience store. Grim didn't tell him that.

It was complicated. Johnny wanted to hurt a dog who had disrespected him at a lake some weeks before. The lake shore was filled with cats, and when Johnny got there only one other dog was around—a spotted tan—holding court with all the prissy cats. The tan had a particular "female feline" all fascinated—the prickly blond Grim had seen—and he had bad-mouthed Johnny in front of her.

"Now, I'm gonna mess up her mind."

"Really?" Grim asked, slurring. His tongue didn't quite work. "What she do?"

"Hey, what she don't?"

"Can't dogs love cats?"

"That's not the point. Some dogs, some cats, sure. You should see her writhing on concrete in the sun. She's paler underneath than I expected. I couldn't believe how pale. And she smelled worse than, well, you."

Grim lowered his head apologetically. He sniffed inside the lampshade. Something was wrong with his nose.

"I'm gonna own that cat. And then I'm gonna own that tan dog."

Grim looked out at the darkening street. In the shadows between the streetlights, bats flew by each other.

"How do I get out of here?"

"Hey," Johnny said, and looked at Grim sideways. "I hate myself, too."

He leapt back into the Jeep and stared out at the street, his ears alert. It was a beautiful cherry-colored Jeep. Grim wanted to jump in it, too, but he was afraid he couldn't jump. And he was afraid of Johnny. He thought Johnny was the devil, even though he knew that couldn't be.

Grim's back itched. He rubbed against the corner of the mailbox until he fell asleep again in a hot sandy furrow at the mailbox's base. He didn't hate anyone. He was glad of that. In his new dream the lampshade became propellers, and he flew above the shadowy bats, who seemed out of control, but who weren't.

Back in Grim's room, Butter took her place in the chair beside Grim's bed. She read an article about a dead horse blocking traffic on the interstate for two hours the day before. She had first read it during the cab ride to the hospital and thought it funny. She stopped reading. Lonnie and Belly Man were still in the hallway talking to the nurses. She didn't know what to do.

She must get back to her job. Christmas break was in two weeks but she would need to go back before then. Or resign. Or get fired. She was tired of teaching. She made little money, and the school often seemed more interested in rules than learning. She was tired of policing children's notebooks for corrected tests, completed homework, and signed study sheets, all sectioned and inserted in the proper prescribed binders. She wanted to create her own school, where kids would be free to create and grow. There had to be a better way—a perfect school that she could create. It was something she had talked with Grim about, and he thought it a good idea. She wanted to go back to school herself, for the credentials and the respect. He was going to help her, he said, and invest in the new school. She had planned to ask her parents to help. Sometimes, when discussing it with Grim, it really seemed possible, and that their partnership might last forever. But now she felt even more restricted, with fewer choices, as if no dream could come true.

Grim lay in half-light. His bed seemed to want to pitch him out. And Butter remembered something Grim had once described for her. His mother had been in the hospital, and Grim was about three years old. He didn't remember why she was there—an asthma attack, or maybe a hysterectomy—he never remembered to ask Rita. But she wore a beaded peach evening dress, tight, like Miss America. The bed floated, levitated. Yet Butter knew it was a false memory. Surely he had merely dreamed it. His mother had not been dressed up. Probably she lay under a sheet that faintly traced her figure. She had been beautiful and remote in that hospital bed. And because Grim was little, the bed rose above him.

Butter turned to find Lonnie and Belly Man standing behind her. Belly Man seemed almost afraid, biting his lip. "You know what it is?" she said. "It's the presence of nothing that's so stunning."

On her face was a look of loathing. Lonnie was pained to see it. It was ugly. One reason he had come was to try to protect her from that kind of damage.

"Well, don't be stunned. Maybe there's something and we just don't know it."

She didn't say anything. Her expression barely changed.

"Oh, yeah," Belly Man whispered. "Like in the movies, you mean. We're surrounded by spirits and we can't see them."

"I don't know if I'm saying all that."

"And maybe they don't know us, either," Belly Man added. "Maybe they can't see us."

"So, then," Butter replied, staring back at Grim, "that explains why we haven't been introduced."

"I saw one this morning," Belly Man said. "I swear it was a ghost, down near the emergency room. The hallway was empty. She had long dark hair and was very, very pale. White, right? And her forehead was bruised purple and a bloody mess. She asked me, 'You had your x-rays, yet?' I said, 'No.' She said, 'I've been waiting a *long* time for mine.'"

Della came in, moving briskly, almost hitting Belly Man

with the door. She saw the struggle on their faces. They had been about to laugh. "I'm sorry," she said, checking dials, her clean white clothes whispering as she worked. "I guess your friends told you. The doctor came while you were downstairs. But he knows you want to see him so he'll probably come back by."

"Shit," Butter swore. Lonnie moved up beside her. He wanted to hug her, but not in front of Belly Man. Della looked at Grim's tubes, wrote something on his chart. She stepped around Belly Man and left.

Belly Man moved closer to the foot of the bed. "This guy is seriously hooked up." Grim took a deep breath. He did that sometimes. Belly Man picked up his chart. He chuckled. "Graham, huh?"

"Yeah." Lonnie smiled. "How about that?"

Butter wished Lonnie would hold her, hoped Belly Man would behave.

"Boo!" Belly Man said, looking down at Grim's shiny smashed face, the white, accordionlike tube in his mouth. "We got your spirits right here, man."

There was only the sound of machines—soft beeps, gurgles, hums. And of breathing.

Wish Lists

THE SATURDAY AFTER they returned from Tampa, Rita had lain in bed all day giving orders. She wanted the house decorated for Christmas. Every now and then, even after all these years, she sniffed the faint funky scent that had permeated the house when they bought it. First they had cleaned, discovering footprints of animals that had tried to climb the walls, as well as decomposed rodents under layers of dust in floor vents. They had found stashes of old acorns in closet corners, behind the stairs, and under loose floorboards in the kitchen. When they turned on the furnace, the sweet dry stench of dirt and decaying animals had fouled the air, mixing with the dense sooty smell that poured out of the fireplace. They fumigated, repaired, painted, and polished. They furnished, cooked, and had parties. They wore the smell away. Almost. So again for this season a pine tree was brought in, scented candles were lit, and cider steamed on the stove. In a minute, she would check on Mayes and the girls.

In the living room Camaro untangled green strands of small colored lights and plugged them into living-room sockets. Most worked. They stretched along the dark gleaming wood floor. Bright, blurry multicolors were reflected in the wood. Camaro guessed her mother was trying to summon Christmas cheer early because of the chill of her grandfather's unmourned death and Uncle Grim's awful accident. The strategy worked for her sisters upstairs in Corvette's room creating Christmas lists. They jumped on the bed and dreamed over catalogues, and Corvette's boom box spread dull thumps of dance rhythms through the living-room ceiling. They had been all the way to Florida without so much as eating an orange or visiting theme parks, water slides, and roller coasters.

Mayes came in with three mugs of apple cider on a red tin tray. Rita was with him. The tray was a holiday prop and Camaro laughed at it. Her father was wearing wide-legged jeans rolled up into four-inch cuffs. "Dad," she said, her look one of critical amusement.

"What?"

"This is silly."

"What is?" He knew. He set the tray on the coffee table beside a cardboard box of decorations. Her mother turned

on lamps. "If I unroll my cuffs, my pants are too long."
He wouldn't criticize Rita about the tray or the cider,
or any of it, even though Christmas depressed him.
He looked at the tree he had put up this morning. It
leaned.

Rita, in white flannel pajamas printed with brown red-
nosed reindeer, stood beside Camaro's favorite lamp in the
house and surveyed the lean of the tree. The lamp, nearly
Rita's height, spiraled up from the floor to a wide tan
shade, now aglow. Camaro thought it a minor marvel, a
puzzle of physics, a straight wiggle. And the light in its
shade was like the gold of summer twilight. She watched
her mother in that light. She thought she was lucky her
mother was alive. The kidnapping had been kept from
the girls, but Camaro understood now. And she imagined
what today would be like if her mother had been killed.
It scared her. She couldn't imagine her father without her
mother. She imagined they would have disappeared; no
one would force them to exist as her mother was doing
today.

Her father sat in the armchair near the wiggle lamp.
The light behind him flowed down the pale gold drape,
thinned and haloed his graying hair. His smooth face
looked tired, circles darker under his eyes. He reached out
to hold Rita's fingers. "I need some medication. Rita, what
do you have that I could use?"

"You don't need medicine. I need medicine."

"I'm depressed. I tell you all the time and you ignore me."

"Tell your doctor, Mayes. What can I do?"

"I do tell him. But I start to laugh and I get no help."

Rita smiled. "You're not doing it right. You have to change your behavior."

"I couldn't do that. You need me. Right? Please tell me you need me. You, too, Camaro."

"We need you." Camaro tugged another string of lights from the cardboard box.

"Get all the girls in here and teach them to say it. 'Oh, Daddy, we need you.' Do that for me."

"Oh, Daddy, we need you," Rita said.

"Thanks. I'm crying out for help, people."

"We'll help you fix the tree, maybe. Then you can help us decorate it."

Camaro connected the untangled strand to one that was already lit. She let the colors flood her vision, the strong pine scent fill her nostrils. She had old parents, she realized. Not really old, but older than those of her friends. What were they thinking, adopting all these young children? Who let them do it? Who would take care of them if something happened to her parents? She remembered a time before Beretta and Lumina came, when Rita and Mayes had taken her and Corvette in a canoe on a river. The boat sat low in the water and there were alligators, huge birds and turtles. Her parents didn't know how to steer the canoe, and Camaro was outraged. Her parents had laughed at her. They couldn't understand how they frightened her—how endangered she knew they all were.

"Just leave the lights on the floor." Mayes flicked his wrist. "Toss the ornaments around the room. That's pretty enough."

Louder thumps sounded from upstairs. Rita looked at the ceiling and sighed. "They will be deaf. Camaro, do something."

But Camaro began unraveling another string of lights. Rita's tone did not mean that Camaro should break up her sisters' pleasure just yet. Mayes pushed to his feet and went to the stereo cabinet under the window. He played Nat King Cole. Rita smiled broadly. She picked up a mug of the cider and sipped, then handed it to Camaro.

"Let's go all the way. Let's have a fire."

"What are chestnuts, anyway?" Camaro asked.

"They fall from the chestnut tree." Rita took another mug.

Mayes turned around and clapped his hands. "I want a drink."

"Oh, Mayes, no, you don't. Straighten up the tree so we can put things on it."

"You know, I never drank all that much. I just always wanted to drink. Not always—just every day. The only reason I stopped drinking was because I wanted to stop wanting. Well I want a drink."

Rita passed him a mug of cider.

"I was never a drunk, merely a drinker." He turned back around to stare out the window. The late afternoon was overcast. Rita and Camaro looked at each other, considering whether Mayes's mood was serious. The music from the stereo swelled, and the sounds from upstairs quieted.

"A miracle has just occurred."

Rita and Camaro held their gazes a second longer. Mayes's tone was so soft now, they thought he could have uttered a truth, perhaps about Grim. And Rita envisioned their parents in love, and Aunt Ruth alive, while Camaro was thrilled with expectation.

"Out there." He pointed outdoors. Rita and Camaro

stepped around furniture to the window. A man they didn't recognize was walking past their house, bouncing on his toes. He swung a bright aluminum walker in one hand.

"That's not funny, Mayes."

"You don't think so?" He put his arm around Rita and smooched at Camaro. "I don't know. I'll bet it is."

Immaterial

IT WAS LATE AFTERNOON. Butter still didn't know anything. Rita and Mayes had yet to call from Durham to check on Grim, and she resented that Lonnie and Belly Man spoke of Grim as though he was dead.

They drank thin vending-machine coffee and snacked on carmel-and-peanut candy bars. Other people got their coffee and wandered back out.

Belly Man said, "Remember when Grim used to ride that yellow horse and wear that black buckskin jacket with the white fringe on it?"

Lonnie answered, "Yeah. I was a kid. That was some corny shit even then. I guess Grim wasn't much more than a kid either. What was he, twenty-something? I mean, whoever heard of such a thing? A black Roy Rogers. We didn't know anything about black cowboys back then. Nat Love. Buffalo soldiers. What's his name, Will Pickett? Maybe Grim did, though."

"I doubt it."

"We used to laugh at him in my house, 'cause he was so country, showing up at parades on that horse with his rope tricks, and advertising for birthday parties. But man, he was impressive, though. The son of a bitch did have a horse, after all."

"I always wanted to be a Indian, myself," Belly Man said. "But he got on TV one time. He was always the coolest dude I ever knew. As far as I know, he never worked *for* anyone."

"Never?"

"Out front on his own the whole time."

"Of course, ever since I actually met him, his front yard was always full of junk cars." Lonnie laughed.

"Hey, well, he had a yard always. Set the standard," said Belly Man.

Lonnie sat quiet a minute, as though reverent in the light of Belly Man's truth. Butter got up from the mustard-yellow vinyl sofa, to give motion to her frustration. She stared for a moment at the photograph of coffee beans on the front of the coffee machine. The beans spilled from a burlap bag. On top of the bag was a steaming paper cup, with the words COFFEE, TEA and HOT CHOCOLATE printed everywhere on it. Which was in the cup, then, damn it, she wondered.

"Do you think Rita will sell the business?" Lonnie finally asked.

Belly Man bit a length of his candy bar. "That girl, Camaro, she can handle it, I'll bet. I'll bet Grim probably willed it to her, anyway. She probably can run it already."

"A heart of gold, Grim. I mean really. We had our rough spots, but a heart of gold. You can attest to that, Belly," Lonnie said, smiling.

"The son of a bitch saved me at least twice."

"I saved your ass, too."

"Naw, my man, you better look at that again."

"It doesn't matter how I look at it."

They were laughing about it, but Butter began pacing the room.

"Anyway, Miss Butter," Belly explained, "when he met you, we were all just rocked. I mean, don't get me wrong; women always liked Grim, because he was free, you know. I mean, he never worked for no white man, and he was just in a good mood almost all the time. But he didn't like just any woman. She had to be special. And, man, when he pulled you, I don't know, I had to hand it to him. I mean, you were the one. What could we do? *You* were so nice. And he dug you to death. We had to be in love with you, too."

"Gee, thanks, guys," Butter stopped behind Belly Man's chair and dug her fingers into his hefty shoulders. She looked at Lonnie. "I love you guys, too."

She sat on the hard yellow sofa. "You have to understand that our good buddy Grim is not dead. He is going to recover because he is strong, and the most human of beings. So why don't you motherfuckers help me plan for the future?"

They didn't respond. As for the future they simply didn't see one for Grim. All you had to do was look at him. Sweet, but wrecked. A brain-damaged invalid at best. Butter regarded them, truly frightened by their vision.

She wanted to tell them what Grim had told her. About when he came here to Tampa to help his dad when the cancer was first diagnosed. The day of the flight there was a weak, disorganized depression far out in the Atlantic, and Grim, as he had told her, noted the irony. For months, depression had been thought the cause of his father's languor. Weariness, loss of appetite, disinterest in the usual diversions of fishing, the Piccadilly cafeteria, *Perry Mason* reruns—classic symptoms.

Grim's stepmother had died three months earlier, in May, discovered dead on the day she was scheduled to see a doctor for persistent gastrointestinal pains. She had spent the night vomiting. Grim's father washed and dried towels and the bathroom rug. He took the cool, damp cloth from her forehead and eased into bed with her. He awoke the next morning in time for the trip to the doctor. His wife looked comfortable, tucked snugly under the soft blue-and-cream comforter she had recently bought. Her skin was cold. His father had reason to be depressed, Grim thought. And the doctors agreed. This was the second wife Mr. Power had lost, the first being Grim's mother, whose mind had slipped away gradually, and long before her will to live—before she chose to drive her car off the interstate and down an embankment into a pond. At least, some people believed she chose it, though it had been ruled an accident.

His father was in the hospital by the time Grim arrived.

He had been dizzy, too weak to walk. A friend, Mr. Goss, had taken him. Low-level oxygen in the blood. Lungs not up to snuff. The doctors gave him hospital oxygen and considered tuberculosis for a time, used that theory to stall, Grim thought. His father knew it was cancer. Grim suspected it. The doctors finally confessed. They started chemotherapy the day before Grim arrived, big doses intravenously, to be spread over three days.

Grim arrived in his father's room twenty minutes before visiting hours ended. Mr. Power was asleep—the nurse had just given him a pill—but awoke long enough to acknowledge Grim's presence. His white-stubbled face was slack from sleep and age. He smiled, lightly shook Grim's hand—held it—and asked about the flight. He drifted off again in the soft blue fluorescence of the night light while Grim described the sparkling, night beauty of Tampa Bay from the sky. The nurse told Grim he could stay as long as he wanted, all night would be fine. But Grim sat only awhile, watched the IV drip, checked whether his father had things he needed—shaving equipment, extra pajamas—and then drove to his father's house.

It was a two-bedroom white stucco with aqua shutters. The porch, a low slab of concrete traced by a wrought-iron rail, needed sweeping. Grim expected the inside to need cleaning, given his father's recent mood. But it was in pretty good shape. It seemed he'd been living in only three of the six rooms; his bed was unmade, the bathroom sink was dirty, and crime magazines cluttered the table beside the sofa in the den. Apparently his father was still reading those despite his depression, and interest he

indulged after retiring from his career as a traveling cigarette marketer and salesman. Grim picked up one showing two tousled blonds in sheared jeans and low-cut,
off-the-shoulder v-neck sweaters. They knelt over a
bound, nearly naked tattooed man; one held a big knife
to his throat. The cover headline read: Deadly Vixens Vex
Florida Police.

Grim straightened the den, made the bed and cleaned
the bathroom. His father had lived in this house twelve
years—since he retired, remarried, and moved to Florida
from Maryland. Grim had visited for his stepmother's funeral. It still felt alien. Before, Grim thought it was because he couldn't share his father's loss of his wife. Grim
felt guilty and resented grieving over this woman who was
not Grim's mother. He stayed two days, despite his father
asking him to stay longer. Tonight it felt as though nobody
belonged in the house. It held no family memories, Grim
realized, none of his family, anyway. The woman who
had decorated it in pastels was dead, and it didn't look as
if a man ever lived there, with its flowered furniture and
pillows. It brought on the old emptiness that thoughts of
his family sometimes induced, thoughts that Grim usually
suppressed.

Grim had breakfast at the Toddle House, drove around,
and then took the interstate to town and the hospital. It
was the last day of the first round of chemo, and Mr.
Power was to go home after lunch. He was anxious to
leave, Grim discovered. Oddly, cancer or no, he intended
to go that weekend to his annual Shriners' dance. He was
feeling much better, he said, and though a little bit pitiful
in the hospital bed, he looked pretty good to Grim. He

no longer had the oxygen tube in his nose. His thin white hair was combed, and his tan scalp was as smooth as the rest of his skin. He had been partially bald for as long as Grim could remember. The chemo wouldn't do much damage there.

When the woman came by with the lunch tray Grim raised the bed and rolled the dining table into place across his father's lap. He lifted the plastic cover—a thrilling moment—and revealed green string beans, yellow squash, brown beef patty, and vanilla pudding. There was a glass of iced tea protected by a crimped-rim, white paper cap.

"Oh, well, want some?"

"Let's see what you don't eat," Grim replied. "If you want to go to that dance, you have to get strong."

"Well, I promised Goss. I think he got me to the hospital just so I'd be able to go."

"You have a date?"

"You, I guess."

The midday news was on the television high on the wall. It showed a map of the Atlantic Ocean where the depression resided. The sound was turned down on the speaker clipped to Mr. Power's pillow, and Grim watched the latitude and longitude numbers appear on the screen, then an address of the TV station for ordering a hurricane tracking map.

"We're getting that," Mr. Power said.

"What? You sent for the hurricane chart?"

"No. What for? We're getting the hurricane."

"It's a tropical storm way out in the ocean somewhere. Eat something, will you?"

Mr. Power balanced a coin of squash on his fork. He

poured Sweet and Low in his tea. "The last hurricane I was in was when I lived in New Jersey. That was a long time ago, after your mother died, the time I left you with your sister. I could only sit in my house and watch trash cans blow by the window."

Grim sat in the green vinyl armchair. He examined the stitching on his boots, and then looked at the framed picture on the wall. It was a farm scene, a barn in a field on a lovely day, unnaturally clear with colors unnaturally bright. It was corny, except that it really was soothing. "Pop, how could you leave me with just Rita?"

"To tell you the truth I didn't know she was sick at the time." He sipped from the bent, flexible straw in the tea. "I really don't think she was. I hear she's doing O.K., now, though. Anyway, she was making me nuts. She was a crazy daughter, not a crazy sister."

"Well, O.K." But she became a crazy sister—manic-depressive, actually, and so afraid of interstate driving that, when Grim was eleven, she drove fifty miles on the shoulder to get to their aunt who had just suffered a stroke. Grim drove home. He was tall enough, and could follow her loopy directions. She put him in charge of most things—cooking, shopping, paying bills. She took a disability leave from the college—though she took in typing for professors and students. She got help and medication, went back to work, and eventually married Mayes. Still, for years, Grim had dreams about headlights shining in his eyes, speeding out of deep black highway space.

Thursday and Friday, after coming home, Mr. Power felt bad—side effects from the chemo. No nausea, for which he had pills anyway—just weakness and an ill feeling that he couldn't describe. Saturday he was up making plans for the Shriners' dance. He took out a tuxedo for Grim. It was old, with wide, peaked lapels. Grim hung it back in the closet and went to make lunch. His father had eaten little over the last two days, but he told Grim that if it wasn't for him, he wouldn't have eaten a thing.

Mr. Power lay down again, and Grim made grilled cheese sandwiches and cucumber-and-tomato salad. He warmed soup from a can. The weather system in the Atlantic had reached hurricane strength. Category one, the weatherman said—eighty miles per hour. The portable black-and-white on the kitchen counter showed its swirl heading west. A hurricane watch for South Florida could be posted by tomorrow. So soon. It was an unpredictable storm. Maybe, thought Grim, it would go away. The weatherman didn't seem concerned; he seemed happy.

Grim peeled the cucumbers, and alternated between hoping that the cancer treatments helped his father and realizing that his father was going to die. It made cooking strange. Knowing and forgetting waved over Grim's consciousness like flags. He imagined his father at three different stages almost simultaneously—young and moving blithely about his life despite children and an erratic wife; brave and sick old man; and dead. Each image hurt. He arranged the food on a white lap tray and took it to his father's room.

"All these crimes," Mr. Power said, indicating the splay of magazines on the bedspread. "I get them on the daily news, in the local newspaper."

Grim set the tray across his father and took a sandwich. He sat in an aluminum lawn chair he had taken from the front porch, because his father found it easier to sit there and dress himself than to stand and do it, or to balance on the uncertain wallow of the bedside.

"Don't some of them happen in Maine?"

"Yeah. Not the good ones. Your child toilet-bowl drownings, your dismemberings, mutilations, serial murders, random drive-by shootings, all right here in the state. Really bizarre stuff. Goss says the country funnels all of its debris down here. It's the last hope of the unhappy. They get here and see no hope at all, and then who knows what they think?"

Grim said nothing. He waited for his father to begin eating. Grim made clinks with his own fork against his salad plate. His dad gave a tight resigned smile and speared a cucumber slice.

He knew his father wanted him to stay in town, but he had only planned a week. Who would want to live in this state, with its weird killers and its killer weather? He hoped Tampa was far enough north not to be destroyed by the storm, but Florida was as risky as earthquake-prone California, another place he couldn't wait to leave when he lived there. At least you can see a hurricane coming; you can get out of the way. It didn't suddenly happen to you, like abandonment. He thought of the propped-up palm trees lining the median of Tampa's interstate expressway. They wouldn't stand a chance in the storm. And what about the poor people in the housing projects and trailer parks he'd seen around the town. What chance would they have?

He watched his father eat the salad and remembered the yellow heat lightning in the black-and-purple sky when he was a kid, when his father and mother were still with him and Rita in Durham. Those were hot and humid nights, his parents drinking cold Pabsts and sitting on the porch in green, slatted rocking chairs, Rita lounging on the slatted swing, the thunder rolling closer—scarier— and his parents saying they *hoped* it would storm, cut the heat. Grim would be afraid to do anything while waiting for the storm, afraid to hop down onto the dark yard even though lamplight from the living-room window filtered out to a small space of grass; afraid to go inside the house and listen to the thunder alone; afraid of the sudden and ultimate crack in the sky, the world falling apart. Tampa, he'd heard, was considered the lightning capital of the world.

He tried to imagine what his father was feeling now, what it was like knowing your days were numbered. Mr. Power had shown Grim where the safe deposit key was kept. He'd told Grim about his will, about some other property nearby. But Grim couldn't move to Tampa. He had his towing and used-car business back home, and Butter. Of course, he could tow and sell cars anywhere. And Butter could probably get a job here if she wanted. He could even marry her, if she wanted, though he wasn't certain. Or he could hire someone to run the business, one of his friends, at least for a month. How much time did his father have, anyway? The doctor had said six months without treatment. But at seventy-seven years old, how long would he live if he beat the disease? How much did it matter?

Something began hitting the roof, intermittent pops. Grim looked at his father but he seemed unaware, intent

on slowly chewing. Whatever it was just kept coming.
"What's that?"

"Children." Mr. Power chewed.

"Whose?"

"They throw rocks at the tangerine tree, trying to
knock down fruit. Then they throw the fruit at each other.
Fruit war."

"But they're hitting the house."

"I have to go out there and beat them sometimes, so
they'll stop."

Grim left to find three boys and a girl taking aim at
the tree beside the house. They were like a Kodak commercial—an Eskimo-looking boy in a red-and-white football uniform; a blond Caucasian boy in green shorts, white
T-shirt, yellow cowboy boots, with black holster and silver
gun; a light brown-skinned girl with frizzy, sand-colored
curls and a mint-green crinoline dress that was too beautiful for play; and a chocolate-brown boy in sky-blue
overalls, one strap undone. They stopped throwing when
they saw Grim standing at the side of the porch.

"You know, you guys ought to get a ladder or something. You're missing that fruit altogether."

"Yeah, well, it's hard to hit a tangerine with a rock,"
the football player explained. His voice was surprisingly
high, like a pretend voice—a cartoon voice.

"I hit one," the girl screamed.

"Yeah, right." When the cowboy turned to sneer at the
girl, Grim could see a small red cowboy hat—too small
for any human's head—hanging on his back from a cord
around his neck.

"*You* don't know. I'm a vision."

"I'm the one that hit something," the brown boy countered.

"What ya'll are hitting is the house."

"The man that lives here don't mind," the girl replied.

"Yes, he does. He said he has to come out here and beat you up, but he doesn't feel like it today. So I'm supposed to do it."

The children didn't say anything for a moment. They looked at each other, grinned skeptically, a little scared. "What's the matter with him?" the football player asked. "We heard he was in the hospital."

"Sick, that's all. He's back home, now. I'm his son."

They giggled.

"What? I can't have a daddy?"

Incredibly, they all shrugged. "You got any children?"

"No. So I don't know much about beating up kids. I guess I'll need a stick or something."

"Nah," the football player said. "Your dad usually just reaches some of the tangerines for us."

"I see." Grim stepped over the rail to the tree. When he picked the green fruit, the strong tangerine scent sprang from the broken stem. It seemed so precious he stopped. "You're not really going to throw these at each other, are you?"

The girl said, "We bowl with them. Sometimes we play hockey."

"And baseball," the cowboy added. "Sometimes we throw them."

There were hundreds of unripe tangerines on the tree. The cowboy kid held open a paper grocery sack, so Grim tossed in a few. "Let me show you something else to do."

He picked three and juggled them. He started small, and gradually tossed them higher until he was looking at them roll green as limes against the sky. The sky was so blue and clear, so sunny and bright. that he marveled at the knowledge of a hurricane out there somewhere, and of his father inside suffering cancer. When the children began to clap, he brought his gaze back down to their level and let the fruit drop cleanly into the sack.

"It's nothing. I used to juggle for a living. I used to do it on a horse. I was a cowboy, like you," he said to the blond kid. He looked at the others. "I played football, too, in school." He glanced at the Eskimo boy. "And I love somebody who is as charming as you. She's a vision, herself," he said to the girl. "Plus, you and me, it's obvious," he said to the other kid. He held out his arm against the boy's. They were almost the same color. "But the first thing I ever got to be real good at was rock-throwing. So listen when I tell you not to hit anybody's house."

Then he roared at them like a lion—another trick. The children took up the paper bag and ran. A couple of them looked back from the street, openmouthed laughing.

Back in the house, Mr. Power was talking on the phone to Goss. He had eaten half of the sandwich, some of the soup and salad. Grim sat in the folding chair and tried a spoonful of soup. It was cold. "Yeah, Grim's gonna be my date. Tell Miriam not to worry about me, because Grim's taking good care of me. He cooks good, too." He motioned for Grim to help himself. "And tell her the hurricane's at least two days away, Goss. Tell her we still have time to have some fun."

Grim picked up the tray from the bed. "I ain't dead

yet," his father said into the phone, and he looked at Grim. Grim took the lunch back into the kitchen. He found a yellow plastic bowl for the leftover soup. A whole set was neatly stacked in one of the bleached-wood cabinets. It was a nice kitchen—beige appliances and beige tile floor. Almond. Airy, spacious, light and clean. A large window over the sink looked onto the green backyard. He could live here, in this house. He'd have to get used to living with thunderstorms—the daily kind—and the flat landscapes, and the flat, pale strip malls. He did like those kids outside; they were pretty cool. He liked the fruit trees, the idea of them. He liked his father.

That night, at eight, Mr. Goss arrived with his wife, Miriam, to pick up Mr. Power and Grim. Goss had an artificial hip and he walked with a cane. Miriam, in a black-and-gold gown, drove. The older men talked about *Perry Mason,* which they watched twice a day. Goss said, "Trag, see, has a name like a space alien. He looks like a space alien."

Mr. Power responded, "It's because he loses all the time."

"He wears his hat cocked to the side, the poor old dude." Goss shook his head. "He fully expects to win. He gloats about every advantage."

"You have to admire his confidence," Miriam said.

"We do," Goss said. "We just can't figure out why he's got any. Him and Berger, another guy with a funny name and an attitude. They ought to get tired of being smacked around by Mason, but they keep trying to smack *him* around."

Miriam said, "They should have canceled this thing. Can you believe we're going to a party with a hurricane coming?"

Grim said, "Like it's 1999."

"Oh, yes, I know that song," Miriam responded. "You're living up to your name, aren't you baby?"

They pulled up at the Holiday Inn. Young men in tuxedos and maroon, gold-tasseled fezzes were there to park the car. Mr. Power and Goss had fezzes, too, and they put them on. The ballroom was set up with white-cloth-covered tables with balloons attached to them. A lot of people were already there. Miriam led, and found their table—number fifty-six—which was on the right about midway into the room, already occupied by two couples.

They were the Reverend and Mrs. Lill and Dr. and Mrs. Dempsey. Rev. Lill, when he stood to shake Grim's hand, was nearly seven feet tall—made taller by the fez he wore. Grim recognized him as one of the ministers who gave a prayer at his stepmother's funeral. It had been a very long, but eloquent prayer. Dr. Dempsey was a chiropractic, and looked closer to Grim's age. He had a square head and face, big square teeth, square shoulders, and looked as wide as he was tall. Their wives looked almost identical—brown-skinned with varicolored, feathered hair. Grim learned they were mother and daughter, that Dr. Dempsey was Rev. Lill's son-in-law.

Everybody left to visit other tables, leaving Grim and his father alone. Next to a dais of Shriner dignitaries, a band was playing Top-40 songs on a stage at the front of the room, but there were fewer musicians than there were instrument sounds, which made the excitement on the stage seem faked. Two young women sat down at the table and smiled at Grim and Mr. Power. Grim didn't know whether to tell them they were in other people's seats. They clutched sequined purses. Each was tall and thin and pretty. They wore their hair short and slicked down in shiny black waves. Their dresses were fitted and lacy, one beige and one royal blue. They seemed to be the only unescorted women in the place.

Just as Grim was hoping they were the guests of Rev. Lill, they got up, thanked Grim and Mr. Power, and disappeared into the maze of tables off to the left. "What I love about black women," Mr. Power said, "is that after you make love with them, after such good fortune, their hair is so different from before you started. It's almost like you create a different woman."

Grim imagined the pressed hair of those girls suddenly fibrilar and wild all over their heads. Then he thought about Phyllis back home, who was as young as those two women, and even prettier. He missed her.

He left to find a pay phone in the lobby. He got her answering machine, and told her he was at a big dance, believe it or not, and he told her he loved her. He hadn't actually told her that before. Now it was on tape. He thought he had sounded pretty sure.

Before he rejoined his father he bought a bourbon-on-the-rocks at one of the portable, white-skirted bars in the corners of the ballroom. Goss and the others had returned from their rounds. "I hope you didn't give money for that." Goss pointed to Grim's drink.

"I was thirsty."

"We're going up to the room. Lodge meeting."

The men left the women at the table. The women seemed glad. They scooted their chairs closer together and started in on a conversation, but Miriam blew them a kiss. Grim followed his father, Goss, Rev. Lill and Dr. Dempsey to the lobby elevator, on which they rose to the fourth floor. Rev. Lill had the key; it was his room.

"Mr. Power and Goss sat in chairs flanking a small oval table by the window. Another table was stocked with bottles of liquor and soft drinks and trays of hors d'oeuvres. Dr. Dempsey sat on one of the double beds, and Rev. Lill stretched out on the other. Grim watched his father, who looked dapper and tired. With a wave of his hand Mr. Power refused a chicken wing that Grim held out to him. "Give me a Sprite."

"You haven't learned a thing," Goss cried. "You gotta eat. You can't just let yourself go."

Mr. Power smiled at Goss. "Goss," he said slowly, "that comment is incompetent, immaterial and irrelevant."

Goss got up and took the wing from Grim. He bit into it. "You're grasping at straws, Power."

Mr. Power and the others laughed. "Son," Mr. Power said. "You are a lucky man to be let in on the secrets of tonight's special Temple meeting."

Grim handed him a plastic cup of Sprite. "I know it. It's an awesome responsibility."

Goss took a drink. "Did you see the titties on the potentate's wife? She's done something to them since the last dance. They look like ready-to-go missiles, now. Aimed and armed."

"Yes." Rev. Lill sighed, lying flat on his back, his hands clasped behind his head and his legs extending over the edge of the bed. "They are spectacular breasts. But these Powers are without women tonight, so it is unkind to tempt them so."

"I don't think they mind,' Goss said.

Dr. Dempsey said, "But you are incompetent, irrelevant etcetera, don't forget."

"You're all taking Power's side just because he has cancer. Let me tell you about the time I was sick. I was announced dead, in fact. Back in 1935, I had to have my bladder stem removed, and they replaced it with the bladder stem of a lamb. I didn't know they were gonna do that. Anyway, when I woke up, I know I smelled a lamb in the room. But I didn't see one. The smell of lamb was all in there, though. Lamb was *all* I could smell. Later a doctor came in and gave me a big orange pill—big around and flat as a quarter. After I took that pill I didn't smell lamb anymore. I was walking home from the hospital when people I knew turned around and went the other way, or ran across the street to hide in some building. Finally I came up on T. J. Jones who told me I was dead. But I was right there looking at T. J. It turns out they had put in the paper that I had died in the hospital, but they had me mixed up with somebody else. It was Donald Gass who had died, not Daniel Goss. I knew Donald Gass, though."

"That's very interesting," Dr. Dempsey said. "What's lamb got to do with it?"

"It represents the average sinner's fear of death. And Goss's incoherence. But I was near death once, myself, in the Army during the war. I had contracted pneumonia and had been in some kind of unconscious trance for days.

One day I came out of it just enough to hear the doctor tell the nurse, 'He's as good as dead as far as I'm concerned.'

"They left the room and I turned to the wall and said. 'Lord, you heard what he said. Now, what are you gonna do? Whatever it is, do it fast. Take me or make me well.' Then I went back into that trance. I heard a low voice say, 'Don't worry, don't worry, don't worry, you're going to be all right, don't worry, don't worry, don't worry.' That voice is what woke me the second time. I looked around but I was by myself. I looked for a loudspeaker for the voice to be coming from, but there wasn't one. I leaned myself over and looked under the bed, because somebody had awakened me with that talk.

"Just then, I heard the nurse's feet come chickety-chickety up the hall. It was a long hall and she always walked in a trot. She came chickety-chickety into the room and held my head in her lap. She said, 'Don't worry, Paul, you're going to be fine. Don't worry, you're going to get well. Just don't you worry.'

"You see, those were the same words I'd heard in my trance. And I got well. The Lord, you see, is powerful, and prayer is powerful, and there are things we don't understand but we mustn't be afraid. Whatever happens, if you trust the Lord, everything will be fine." He cut a glance over at Mr. Power. Mr. Power looked pleasant.

"Good gracious, Paul. I see you're trying to show me up with that religious twist, but your story makes no more sense than mine."

"Some of you fellows have wives downstairs," Mr. Power said.

"And Goss wants to slow dance with the potentate's wife." Dr. Dempsey laughed.

"I just want to understand her titties."

"Meeting's over, then. Get your drinks, boys." Rev. Lill stood up from the bed. "Grim, all this can be yours. We invite you to join our brotherhood under the noble sponsorship of your father. No pressure. We do a lot of good, despite what you've witnessed tonight. You, too, are a good man. That's why you're welcome."

"Thank you, Rev. Lill." He looked over at his father sipping Sprite and peeping over the cup. There really were such things as smiling eyes. The rest of the men stood and gathered their fezzes. Rev. Lill's massive body blocked the door while he poured and tossed down a shot of Scotch. He winced. "Spirits," he said, and winked down from his height at Grim.

When they got home, Grim finally reached Butter on the phone. Everything was fine. She had been downtown at a conference all evening. But she was worried about him and his father. She wanted to know what they were going to do about the hurricane. Wouldn't they need to evacuate? Why didn't Grim bring his father to North Carolina tonight? He told her he had been invited to join the Shriners.

"You want to join the Shriners?"

"Not really."

"Then what are you talking about? Get out of there."

The next day, Mr. Power wouldn't get out of his pajamas. By midmorning the hurricane was at category three and South Florida was under a hurricane warning. The news showed people in Miami boarding up windows and hauling small boats away from harbors. The storm was predicted to hit land around midnight. Nobody could predict for Tampa. It remained under a watch, and people were buying extra water and canned goods.

Grim made a tuna salad. He found a hurricane lamp and fuel in a closet, but it had no wick. He filled pitchers and jars with water, but he thought he should get more. And there weren't enough fresh batteries in the house for the flashlights and portable radio.

He went to three grocery stores. The parking lots were packed. All the grocery carts were in use and the checkout lines backed halfway down the grocery aisles. There was no bread, no water, no beer. Only double-A and triple-A batteries were left on the revolving display racks. People were edgy.

Grim drove to a mall. He went into Sears looking for a 6-volt battery, but they were sold out. He found one at a sporting-goods store. At a candle shop, though people crowded the small store, the proprietor put his arm around Grim, led him to a wall of wicks, and picked out the kind he needed. It was a fragrant place. Warm light glinted off the lamp glass and the smooth candle surfaces. Grim bought some candles.

He still had to get D-cell batteries, and he found them at a building-supply store next to the mall. Only the store's own brand remained, but they had plenty. He bought a dozen D-cells, a dozen C-cells, and some large plastic jars for keeping extra water. He stood in line where a family in front of him and a family behind spoke past him excitedly in Spanish or Portuguese. Their shopping carts overflowed with bags of potting soil, sheets of plywood, batteries, blue air-conditioner filters, lumber. The orange-aproned checkout woman told him, "I never want to sell another battery as long as I live."

He had been out most of the day. His father was asleep on the sofa in the den. Grim made a big dinner of fried chicken, macaroni and cheese, and green beans—something to last a couple of days. He planned to fill a cooler with ice and perishable food if the power went out.

He woke his father and made him eat, then he put batteries in the flashlight and radio. He got the oil lamp working, filled the jars with water, and had his father call Goss to see if he needed anything—but Goss was all set. The only thing left to do was to wait.

They watched television, and between shows the weather reporters kept changing the prediction about when the hurricane would land. It was a powerful storm, they said—category four, 160-mile-per-hour winds. It would hit Miami sometime between midnight and dawn, and who knew what it would do after that? Climb up to Tampa? Skip across to the gulf and Louisiana? Diminish?

Mr. Power went to bed at eleven o'clock. He took a pill prescribed to help him relax. Grim called Butter. He wanted to talk about his day, his frustration, his fear of the storm. He said how amazing it was to know something bad was on the way but to have the world around you seem at ease. The television reporters, for instance, were making jokes. Butter said that was because it was their job, and that people were at ease because they couldn't imagine how bad the worst could be. Then she said she was sorry, she just wanted him home, she wanted them to be holding each other.

Grim wanted to bring up the idea of moving to Florida. It was too soon; he wasn't sure. For all he knew, there would be no Florida after tonight. He promised to call her tomorrow to let her know he was safe. And he did. Tampa was unharmed the next morning. The sky was a strange, bright pewter, but there was hardly a strong breeze. It was peculiarly sunny—silvery. The Kodak children, because school had been closed, played in the street in front of the house.

It wasn't until the next day that he saw pictures of Miami's destruction. Miles of property had been crushed. People had died. Zoo animals—giraffes and monkeys— ran wild in the streets. People roamed about looking for their homes. Butter was right; no one could have imagined it. And it seemed to Grim that Tampa could not quite believe its good luck. People looked slightly dazed, guiltily happy, but sad, too, as if a bullet had whizzed by and hit the guy behind them, as if someone else's daughter were the victim of the serial killer.

It took another two long days for Grim to contact various support agencies to find someone to cook and clean for his father. Miriam helped. His father could get a nurse. Goss could drive him for his medical checkups. Grim took him in for the first scheduled visit, and the blood levels were O.K.; he was having an easy time with the chemo. His remaining hair would be gone in a week. And in four weeks he would have to go back into the hospital for the second dose. So far, his x-rays showed no change in the cancer, but according to the doctor, that was good news —it hadn't spread.

Still, Mr. Power seemed depressed. He had expected the cancer to recede. On the ride home Grim suggested they go to the beach. Why not? The hurricane was gone. The beach was calm. Really, there was nothing they could do about the devastation down south. And this was Grim's last day.

"I've already missed *Perry Mason*. You'll like the beach. The women, you'd be shocked at what they wear." Grim felt like crying. His father amazed him ... always had, in one way or another.

They got Goss to come along, too. Miriam had to work at her part-time job at a department store, but on her suggestion, they drove to Sarasota. It wasn't too far, and Mr. Power and Goss waded in the turquoise surf while Grim sat on a lawn chair on the bright sand. Colorful sails drifted by and the occasional yacht came into view off the horizon. People lounged and swam, as though the hurricane hadn't happened, hadn't even threatened. Grim tried to read a crime magazine, but kept looking at a young couple in radiant swimwear throw a green translucent Frisbee.

A lifeguard drove by on a three-wheel motorbike, and stopped down shore to peer through binoculars at the gulf. He blew his whistle, but Grim couldn't see what the problem was. He thought drowning victim first, then shark. His father and Goss began wading in the direction of where the lifeguard pointed, as though the lifeguard wanted people to go there, and then Grim noticed a wide darkness floating in the water. Some of the people on the shore moved down to the water's edge while some in the water got out. The darkness was a large, formless shadow under the waves, like an oil slick, or a cloud of poison ink, some hazard let loose by the hurricane.

Grim stood and motioned for his father to come out,

but he and Goss kept walking toward it. Maybe it was a large school of fish, Grim thought, until a blunt rubbery-looking tip of the thing broke the surface and quickly re-submerged. An old raft? Still, Grim trotted down closer to his father and Goss to yell for them to get away—don't walk toward the thing, for heaven's sake.

Groups of people joined Mr. Power and Goss, waded up beside the darkness, some with 35mm and video cameras. They gathered around and escorted it past where Grim stood. His father waved him into the surf, and Grim flowed in near the back of the entourage beside a large blond man holding a small movie camera. "What is it?" Grim asked. The man smiled brightly and answered casually and profusely in what sounded like German. Grim trudged away, trying to catch up with his father at the front of the group slowly making its way up the coast.

Suddenly, several knobby, rubbery tips protruded from the blob and sank again, and then it made a swift flowing movement to reverse itself, bringing the crowd back toward Grim. "Don't touch," someone shouted. "It may be against the law."

"Manatees!" a woman said. "Endangered! It's incredible!"

The German man answered her in his language, and she laughed excitedly, "Yes, yes, yes. Seven altogether!"

Swiftly, they turned again, passing right by Grim's legs. He was with his father and Goss, now. Their shoulders shone in the sun. He walked with them a ways while Goss guessed the reasons for the manatees. Warm currents. Lost. Hurricane. Mr. Power said, "Goss, it's immaterial." Goss touched one.

When the crowd grew larger and the walk took them far from their lawn chairs on the beach, Grim dropped out and went back to shore. He watched until he could no longer distinguish his father and Goss. It was amazing his father had the energy for such a walk. And Goss was out there with his bad hip. He hoped they'd be back before sundown, because Miriam had said the sun turned red-orange and beautifully lucent, and actually melted into the water like candy. He wanted to see that with his father, to see if it was true, gather further evidence and further hope that anything at all could happen.